8 Second
Decision

HJ Bellus

Ride hard—
♡ my
Bellus

8 Second Decision

Dedication-

To my #ROOTS. Never forget who you are and where you came from...

"From the soil that nurtured them to the love that made them blossom...always follow your roots."

Chapter 1

Merek

"Who the hell is she?"

"Back in town for—what?—two hours, and already scoping out a fresh piece of ass, Merek?"

I just raise an eyebrow to my little brother, give him that sly Slatter grin, and toss back my longneck.

"Maybe."

"New waitress. Been here about four months. About the time you left for Houston and traveled on down the road riding them bucking horses."

The tension is evident in my little brother's voice, with ample amounts of jealousy laced in there. His loyalty has always been to the ranch, Daddy's legacy and Momma's heart, and I've been the wildcard. Chasing my dreams eight seconds at a time on the road. I love the ranch and the rich history it holds deep in the soil of the grounds, but I'm more of my granddad's type, wild at heart and addicted to the rodeo lifestyle.

"Yeah, four months, Marvel, and I'll be home for the next three. Get over yourself."

"Daddy's not doing good and—"

I cut his arrogant ass off before he has the slightest chance of giving me his tired-ass sob story. "I send money home. I've kept shit afloat, and if you ever insinuate that I'd let Granddad's ranch go to hell, you can fuck off."

Marvel receives my message clear as day and the subject changes quite rapidly.

"Fall calves look real good. Prices are high too." Marvel sips on his whiskey.

I nod at the information and would be lying to myself if I said I didn't miss the ranch. I'll just never know if there's a true balance between chasing that buckle and living on the ranch. Granddad always did it until his body broke down and forced his hand. He's the only reason I look forward to coming home. Long talks with him always seem to help ground my ass.

"Anyway, what's her name?" I ask again while staring at the new waitress.

Well, at least new to me. She's kind of hard to miss with her long, tan legs strutting about in her tight, white shorty shorts. God damn, there's something about her long brown waves of curls that makes me want to take her on the bar. I readjust myself and try to focus on Marvel rambling on about ranch shit. It's the same old story. Our dad has blown the majority of earnings on horse racing. He calls it his hobby, but in reality it's going to be the death of the Slatter legacy.

I don't miss the quick glances she keeps sending my way either. Her bright green eyes flash over to me as Marvel keeps talking and I keep drinking. The way I see it, the faster I drink, the quicker I get her cute little ass over here to serve me.

"Dickface, have you listened to a word I've said, or just scheming your game plan to get down her pants?" Marvel tosses the basket of peanuts into my chest, causing nuts to fly everywhere.

"I'm fucking listening." I toss back the rest of my drink and raise the empty longneck.

She spots me and signals with a nod.

"What are we going to do? Dad owes a bunch of people money."

"Well, calf prices are good and I've got money in the bank." I relax back into my seat, kicking out my long legs. "We'll handle it like we always do."

"Something has to give, Merek. Granddad's heart can't take much more, and you know Momma, she'll never say a word."

I shrug off Marvel's concern. He's always been the bleeding heart in the family, trying his damnedest to restore everything to the ways of our childhood. Our oldest brother, Maverik, is a lot like me and does a lot of shoulder shrugging.

"Did you need something?" A sexy as hell voice invades our table.

Turning my head, I come face to face with a green-eyed beauty and actually stumble trying to talk.

"What did you need? Or is it just normal to wave beer bottles at women?" She plants her hands on her hips, glaring down at me.

I can't help but flash my wicked grin back at her. Now that she's closer, her eyes are a piercing green and her skin a stunning olive tan. I try not to stare, but I seem to be pulled into her. Marvel throws an elbow into my ribs. "Quit wasting her time, Merek."

"Sorry." I shake my head quickly. "Another beer."

"That's it?" Her long brown hair whips over her shoulder.

My cocky meter hits an all-time high with the mixture of her voice and attitude toward me. "Yeah, that's fucking it."

"Well, next time, march your happy little ass up to the bar and order."

I catch sight of her rather large silver buckle resting below her sliver of skin that's showing. It's a state champion buckle and one that's near elusive to win in Texas with such stiff competition. As she walks away, I can't help admire her backside as well.

"Never seen a girl get to you that fast, little bro." Maverik pulls out a chair, swings it backward, rests his forearms on the back, and settles in. His best friend, Jake, a black and white cow dog settles underneath him. They're inseparable. Jake was a birthday present from Granddad for Maverik's tenth birthday. All of us boys were damn jealous of that beautiful pup. "Order me a drink, bitch."

Maverik glares down at Marvel and then slugs him in the arm. Marvel doesn't even argue because he knows it's one argument he'll lose. I let out a loud laugh and send a head nod to my older brother.

"Back in town, uh?"

"Yep, three month break. Figured I'd come raise hell around here."

"Good, we missed your ugly ass. Did you bring me any puss home?"

I toss the empty peanut basket back at him. "Naw, man, you'll have to stick to hometown puss for now."

"Asshole." Maverik slings the napkin dispenser toward my side of the table.

A longneck amber brown bottle slams down on the table with gold liquid sloshing down the sides. "Here's your beer, Champ."

I look back up into the lustful green eyes that seem to love to glare back at me. Not an ounce of amusement rests on her face this time. Damn, I was hoping to pique her curiosity just a bit, and it's clear someone filled her in on who I was. Well, it's about time she understands who she's dealing with.

I rise to my feet and close the space between us. I feel her move back until she's up against a wall, and I follow her until our bodies are softly pressed into each other.

"I'm not Champ. I'm Merek." I run my palm up the skin of her arm, leaving goose bumps behind. "But I can make you feel like a champ. Just give me one night."

I watch as her eyebrow rises in curiosity and I know I have her right where I want her. I fall further into her, listening to our buckles scrape together and then run my hand right back down the same path.

"Meet me outside after your shift." My palms settle on her hips and I'm surprised how she doesn't fight me touching her. "What's your name, gorgeous?"

I watch as she breaks into a fit of laughter under my touch. Tears begin trailing down her cheeks as she tries to calm her howls. Her hands settle onto my chest, and the next thing I know I'm being pushed back down into my seat with more force than I would've expected the little bombshell to have.

"My name is Challis and I'll break it to you easy. You don't stand a fucking chance with me, Champ."

She turns to walk away, leaving me with my jaw on the motherfucking floor, and then I do what I do best, play the dick card.

"How many guys did you have to blow to get that buckle?"

My words stop her mid-stride, but she doesn't turn around to battle back. Instead, I watch as she lifts both arms and sends me the bird over her shoulder. And my God, if her little action didn't cause my jeans to get tighter where they shouldn't be.

My brothers' roars of laughter drag my attention from Challis's ass sauntering away from me.

"Damn, I've never seen a woman do that to

Merek." Maverik grips his hat waving it in appreciation toward Challis and her turn-down.

"How's it feel, asshat?" Marvel stares me down.

"Shut the hell up, I was just dicking around with her." I toss back half of my beer before coming up for air. "I can get a piece whenever or wherever."

Maverik leans up on the table, firmly planting his elbows down. "You did notice her buckle was for chasing cans, so I'm pretty sure she didn't have to suck any dick for it."

My eyes widen trying to recall exactly what her buckle had on it. The letters for the state association are the only things I can remember.

"Nah." I shake my head from side to side. "There's no way in hell some state champ is in here bartending and not rodeoing for a living."

"Here she comes." Marvel slaps my arm. "Look."

Challis passes our table quite swiftly, but I catch sight of the barrel racing decorating her buckle and the year. Well, if it's hers she's about four years younger than me, yet a bit older than Marvel.

"She's Challis Jones. Remember old man Jones from Fulton County?" Maverik watches me, waiting for a light bulb to go off. "Wine Cup Ranch, the godfather of bucking bulls."

Then it hits me. "She's a Jones?"

"She's not just a Jones. She's Cody Jones' only child, and a daughter at that."

I shudder thinking about the heir of Cody Jones in the same bar as me. Country roots don't get any deeper than Cody Jones. He lived and breathed everything rodeo until he was buried six feet under. My body shakes remembering the gruesome details of the accident.

10

"What the fuck is she doing here? She's at least a good couple of hundred miles from home."

"Who knows?" Marvel shrugs. "She's kept her distance from everyone in town."

"So, she just rambled in one day and lives in the alley?" My frustration level is evident in my voice, and I'm done waiting for answers.

"Still an asshole." Maverik relaxes back in his chair, avoiding eye contact with me. "Lives with her aunt out at Lazy Hat Ranch."

"Tori, the one who owns this place?"

"Yep, I guess that's her aunt," Maverik replies.

"Tori is related to Cody." I tip back the brim of my cowboy hat and lightly scratch my head, struggling to put the puzzle pieces together.

"Yeah." Maverik stands, downing the last of his drink. "No one knows her story and she's never come across friendly enough for anyone to be brave enough to ask. I have a party waiting for me. Later, pussies."

Before I can ask another question, Maverik is heading toward the door where a brunette awaits him while his faithful companion, Jake, trails right behind. I shake my head wondering if things ever change. Maverik is a playboy at heart and as the years pass it seems he'll never settle down. He had one true love who broke him, and I don't think he's capable of ever loving again, but my thoughts quickly go straight back to analyzing Challis. I'm not bashful about staring her down or studying each of her movements.

"Let's go." Marvel slaps my arm. "I'll go pay the tab and get the truck."

I just nod to him as I continue staring down the

beauty behind the bar, appreciating each of her moves and the way her hair dances up and down her back as she pours drinks. Against my better judgment, I stride up to the bar, continuing to stare her down, and apply a bit more pressure with my presence.

"What?" Her voice is filled with displeasure.

"Another beer."

"Your brother just paid the tab." She points toward Marvel at the end of the bar. "Time to go."

"I'm a big boy." I adjust myself before sitting on the barstool and don't miss the fact her view seemed to appreciate every single movement.

"Fine." Challis whirls around, snags a beer from the tub of ice behind the bar, and sends it sailing across the bar top toward me. I catch her wrist with one hand before she has the chance to escape and the chilled beer bottle in the other.

Staring into her green eyes, I feel chills run up and down my spine. "I just wanted to say nice to meet you, Challis Jones."

I let go of her wrist and am surprised not to see her bolt. She stands straight up, rubs her wrist. "Wish I could say the same back to you, Champ."

I relax back onto the barstool, holding my cold beer to my chest. "In time, Challis. In time, you'll be impressed."

"Fuck off." Challis turns on her heels, whirling her long brown hair in the air and is off.

I try not to stare at her and keep pleasantly distracted with hometown people coming up and welcoming me home. Soon a large crowd settles in around me as we shoot the breeze. Challis remains cold and distant toward me and the people surrounding me.

"Merek, you're home."

Craning my neck I see Madison Nicholson standing behind me bouncing up and down on her toes. I flash her a grin and tip my hat to her and then extend my arm out to her. I feel her fingers wrap around my hand as I pull her into me. Bodies part to make room for her, and I can't help but smile when I look up at her.

Madison and I were high school sweethearts at one point in time. But it was evident our paths were never going to mesh, so we settled for fuck buddies when the time was convenient for both of us.

"Home from doctor school?" I ask her, brushing her blonde locks from her face.

"Duh, winter break."

"Excuse me, smarty pants." I slap her ass, making her squeal.

She leans in, resting her hand on my chest. "Got plans tonight, Merek?"

"I think I just made some." I wink at her.

Without warning, Madison leans down and places a kiss on my lips. It's light and sweet just like her. Out of the corner of my eye, I catch Challis staring at us, so I pull Madison in, deepening the kiss. A loud crash rings out in the small bar, and when I look up, I see the front door slamming and Challis is gone.

Chapter 2

Challis

My small room is stuffy, and I toss and turn in my rumpled sheets for about the tenth time. My alarm clock flashes red numbers back at me. Four a.m. I still can't stop thinking and relax just enough to fall into a peaceful state of slumber.

I've stayed strong since Daddy's death. I even came home from rodeoing to help save the ranch my wicked stepmother is losing, only to be escorted from it by the local sheriff.

Thank God for Aunt Tori welcoming me into her home. It's no family secret that she and my dad never got along, but she always had a soft spot in her heart for me. Even if she claims her only sibling was a dick.

I rip the last sheet from me, slamming my palms down into the mattress, and feel the goose bumps fucking Merek Slatter inflicted on me earlier. If the cocky asshole thinks he'll have me falling at his boots he has another thing coming. I have exactly four months to make enough money to buy my daddy's ranch back from Satan herself.

There's no room in my life for a sexy cowboy, even if his name is Merek Slatter. I did my best to play off even knowing who he was, but Jesus Christ, even the cactus in Texas know who Merek is. He's Texas' pride and joy. Not only is he one hell of a bareback rider, but he also has the personality and looks to capture the hearts of hundreds.

I press my palms into my forehead, cussing myself out for even knowing this much about the man. I've waited weeks for him to come strolling into the bar since his brothers are some of my aunt's best customers. I knew the day would come where he'd make an appearance. It was only a matter of time. In the rodeo world he's Donald Trump—everyone watches him closely.

I met Merek one year at the state rodeo when he was a senior and I was an upcoming freshman. He flirted with me, making my ovaries cry, and then continued on down the trail of girls following him. From tonight's display with the little blonde, it looks as if some things never change. When his lips devoured hers, something inside me burst, and I still can't pinpoint it. I know it's the reason I can't sleep. My temper is one thing that's never been on my side.

I don't know if it's the fact that Merek is on top of the world with everything he needs or that he thinks he can have anything he wants at the drop of a dime that set me off tonight. Well, tonight he stepped in front of the wrong cowgirl thinking he can have his way with.

It's mentalities like these that took my daddy down and allowed the snake of evil in our lives. My daddy was on top of the world in the rodeo business, but it all ended the night of his wreck.

I sit up, throwing my feet over the side of the bed, letting them dangle on the cold tile floor. I find the ponytail holder on my wrist and pile my hair up in a messy bun and then search my room for my running shoes. The moonlight shining in through the window lights up the room perfectly.

After I'm dressed to go for a run, I catch a glimpse of movement out my window. Peering out, I see my best friend standing in the circle corral strong and steady in his posture. Teebaby, my horse, my partner in crime. He's mainly white but has several black markings all over him, and every time I see him I feel at home. My fingers have braided and unbraided his black mane and tail countless times. I've memorized the different patches of colors covering his body. The horse that has never let me down and is going to help me win back the ranch. My daddy gave me Teebaby on my thirteenth birthday and we've been unstoppable since.

My fingers outline his silhouette on the pane of glass. We were well on our way to being collegiate champs when Daddy was in his accident. It didn't matter how close we were; there was no option but to come home and take care of him.

My thoughts tend to spiral very quickly out of control, so I decide to slip from the house and go for a run. Aunt Tori doesn't live too far from town, so I steady my pace and pound away my worries, hoping to exhaust myself enough to eventually find sleep when I make it back to Tori's.

***

"Go running again last night?" Tori flips the egg she's frying.

"Yeah, sorry if I woke you up." I run my fingers along the hem of the lace tablecloth lost in thought.

"I just don't like when you run at night, Challis."

"I couldn't sleep, and sometimes it finally helps me fall back to sleep."

"And did it work last night?" She raises an eyebrow while pointing her spatula at me.

"Nope."

"Did that Merek Slatter get you all hot and bothered, sister?"

16

"Ewww. You mean the walking and talking STD? And that's a big ass no."

"I don't believe you."

"Well, too bad. It's the truth." I stand to fix my plate of breakfast. "I got a notice about the ranch stating my time window went down to twenty days to make the payment or Lola can sell."

Tori lets out an audible gasp, and no matter how much she and Daddy hated each other, I know, deep down, their bonds are tight.

"Well, looks like we'll be selling another group of calves then."

"No." I slam down my plate on the chipped countertop. "I'm not making you do that."

"You're not." Tori steps up in my face. "They're your daddy's cattle, and since I despise the bastard, I despise them. We are selling them and that's final. Eat your breakfast then go hook up the trailer."

I don't argue with her and instead I begin to fill my plate with a protein packed breakfast. Aunt Tori puts up a tough game face, but deep down, I know she's nothing but all about family at the end of the day, and refusing to sell her and daddy's calves would be a slap in the face to her. Sometimes in life you just have to bite down on your tongue and accept what's being given to you.

"Good slop, Auntie. Going to hookup the gooseneck. Meet me out front in fifteen."

The Texas sun pounds down on my skin, warming even the coldest of emotions built up in me. Tori's place is nothing compared to mine and Daddy's back in the day. Green panels lay strewn over and empty rusty water tanks litter the corrals. Her place can be categorized as a once been and now a mere ghost town.

Daddy and Tori's sibling war has been nothing but public news. She was booted with a hefty check when their father died and has never let the grudge go. My daddy was always in the spotlight in the rodeo world and ranch life. Being a single dad never hurt his credit, and his killer looks just added to his trouble. Tori would take me for a couple of months in the summer while my daddy traveled up and down the road, and I still don't remember a time where the siblings were civil to each other.

"Mornin', Teebaby." I sneak him a couple treats through the panels and nuzzle in as close as I can.

He's my best friend, brother, soul-person, or whatever you want to call it. His mane has caught many of my tears and shared in the pain of heartbreak I've experienced. He's won me buckles and shared in endless celebrations with me. Teebaby has witnessed the ups and downs with me and has never ever turned his back or judged. Again, he's my best friend.

I pat him on the forehead, lean in, and place a kiss on his nose. "We are off to sell one more calf. Here's hoping between that and our rodeo money, we'll be home before you know it, baby."

Teebaby's understanding eyes make my knees buckle, but it's when he nuzzles back into my touch that I know he's there forever. "Got to go, baby. We'll be on the road next weekend. We need big money."

I drag my zebra striped boots to the truck as I think of my daddy's words when he gave me Teebaby.

'Baby girl, the day will come when you have to let this horse go. It won't be easy and will more than likely

rip your heart out. And you may find it possible never to love or get attached to another horse after having your heart broken. But cherish the times of loving and living that you have on the back of this beautiful paint horse of yours. Are you ready for the ride of your life, Challis Bug?'

There's not much that I've argued with my daddy on until Teebaby, and that's because he'll always be mine, and the day he quits running barrels is the day I retire. My daddy never shed a tear or blinked an eye when it was time to put an animal down on the ranch, even his favorite horse. Deep down, I hope it was just him being brave for me or some macho man shit, because I know there's no way in hell I'll ever be able to fill his boots on that end of the spectrum.

I decided on hopping in my Dodge Cummings instead of Tori's since I know exactly how to back it up and love the roar of the engine zipping down the road. I won the truck my freshman year of college and it's been the one thing I refuse to sell to save the ranch. It's an obnoxious lime green color with several ads down the bed, but it's all mine and always will be.

Carefully, I reverse my beast back to the gooseneck trailer knowing exactly when to stop. My phone lights up on the console and when I see the number flashing across the screen I fight to keep my breakfast down. It's Lola, the bitch spawn of Satan, who managed to weasel her way into my daddy's life, marry him while I was away at college, and then somehow sent him to his grave.

She's beyond eager about selling the ranch and riding off into the sunset with some young Brazilian boy to fulfill her every fantasy. I've never felt like trash until the day I witnessed my daddy marry her.

Being an only child whose mother never wanted them, and then some Wild West cowboy as a father, I was attached, bonded, and sealed to him.

The only day I saw my daddy cry was the day I drove west to college. Looking back, it's as if that was his true burial and funeral, because from that day nothing added up. Lola came into his life and wrecked it—plain and simple.

I easily slide my finger across the screen, accepting the call and then hanging up immediately. She knows where I stand, as I do her. If my daddy taught me anything it was never give up on what you believe to be true. I know one way of life, and that's the ranch in Fulton and rodeo. And that's exactly what I'll go down fighting for.

Tori waves like wild as I ease the truck back into the trailer. I've done it a thousand times and could probably even execute it drunk and blindfolded to boot. Not wanting Tori to mess up her bad back any further, I hop out quickly to attach the trailer to the truck.

"Get in, Tori, I got this."

"The calves are over in the G lots and all ready to load."

Everything inside of me wants to usher her ass to her side of the truck but knows the deviant little shit will refuse. "Got it...go."

I begin twirling the hitch, settling it down on the ball, connecting the trailer to the truck. All of these actions come second nature as Daddy always taught me at a young age to work my ass. His words ring clear as a bell in my head. *'You're a girl and everyone thinks girls can't do shit, Challis, so I don't care how hard of a task it is...you'll do it.'*

Climbing back into the truck, I peer over at Tori whose eyes are glazed over. "Are you sure you want to sell the last group of cattle on your ranch, Tori?"

"They were never mine, Challis. Your daddy always had the upper hand."

Growing up, I could handle the back and forth and Tori's bitter words toward my father, but something clicked the day we had to lay him to rest and now the words don't settle so well with me.

Instead of arguing or engaging in a round of twenty questions, I back up to the loading chute, glide down my aviators, and hop out once again and go to load the remaining sixty head of cattle on my aunt Tori's ranch. I know it's the selfish side of me coming out to play, but these plump black beauties will definitely bring in a pretty dollar.

"I'll get them corralled and loaded. Stay here." I give Tori a sideways glance as I set the emergency brake. "And play pinochle or whatever the fuck you old lizards do."

I spot Teebaby running back and forth across the circle corral and his excitement is nearly contagious. Teebaby is always ready to hit the road and perform. He's so damn smart. He sees me, the truck and trailer and is ready to roll. My vision darts directly to the corrals because it's too painful to ignore my best friend.

The sound of his hooves pounding the dirt as he runs up and down his pen breaks my heart. Hopping over the fence, I jog toward him but stop in the barn first to snag him his favorite treat.

When I finally get to him he's amped up and breathing hard from pacing his pen.

"Here, baby." I offer him a cookie and feel the palm

of my hand get slimed as he inhales it. "I'm just going to town. No rodeo today."

I give his cheek one more pat before I wrap my arms around his neck and squeeze. "Just cattle going on the trailer today. Maybe a ride later tonight."

I break from his pen because I know I could stay in there all day and talk to him, which would lead to saddling him up and then finding the nearest arena to practice running barrels.

Loading cattle is easy and another job I could do blindfolded. Dealing with eight hundred pound calves is nothing compared to the one-ton bucking bulls I had to work with for Daddy.

"That was fast." Tori stares over at me as I jump back into the truck.

"I even gave Teebaby a treat."

"I knew you would."

I smile over at her and drive down the dirt lane. I mindlessly pay attention to her directions to the Silver Star Ranch. I chuckle at the prestigious name.

"What are you finding so damn funny, Challis?"

"Just the ridiculous name...I mean why not Shining Silver Star? It's just a cocky ranch name."

She lets out a grunt of disapproval and goes back to playing pinochle on her phone. Reaching over I turn up some Miranda Lambert and drive to the other side of town.

When we pull into the ranch's driveway, its name definitely fits it, and I even hate to admit that it may be the prettiest piece of land I've ever seen. The long paved lane is framed by perfect white fencing on each side. Knee high, lush green pastures wave in the breeze, filled with gorgeous horses of all colors.

As we get closer, the barns are fancier than most

homes back where I live. And the mazes of fencing become more intricate the closer we get to the center of the ranch. A mansion comes into view, or rather a four-story castle with several smaller homes surrounding it.

"Do you know where we are supposed to go, Tori?"

"Merle said go to the red barn with double white doors and back in there."

"Got it," I say as I spot one of several barns with that matching coloring, but this one has a row of feed bunks and several pens with feeder cattle in them. There is a wide opening, making it easy to back up to the cattle chute.

"You sure you want to sell the last of your cattle, Tori?"

"Yep." She nods and then hops from the truck. "You need your home, and I'm going to help you get that, missy poo-poo."

"I should slap you for using that name. You know I hate it."

"And you know I love calling you it." She slams her door and takes off to find someone in charge.

I slide from the cab of the truck and inhale the fresh air and admire the gorgeous scene before me. The sun is out with a clear blue sky, and there's a crisp and refreshing bite to the slight breeze.

"Can I help you?"

The deep voice startles me as I whip around to see where it's coming from. Merek Slatter stands before me with his hands perched on his hips, with his sweaty chest on display, and his straw hat pulled low. My heart fucking thuds when I see the god before me, but I do everything in my power not to show any weakness.

"What are you doing here, Challis?"

I try to talk and again nothing comes out. My eyes zero in on the dabbles of sweat beads running down his chest straight into his v-line, and then disappearing into the waistband of his jeans.

"I'm Tori, and I talked to Merle about selling a lot of calves to him." Tori pats my shoulder and walks past me.

I'm left with my jaw on the edge of dropping wide open from the sight before me.

"Yeah, that's my dad. I can take care of you."

Oh, I'm thinking he can take care of me in more ways than one.

I take a step back and try my best to block out his deep voice as the two of them talk business. He was such an ass last night, mind you a hot ass, but still an asshole. Yet in the light of the day and in the middle of hard work, he's the thing that makes panties instantly combust.

"Challis, help Merek here unload the calves."

"Um, yeah." I round the front of the truck and walk back down the other side of it to avoid any more contact with the man.

Merek's at the back of the trailer trying to unlatch it, but little does he know there's a trick to it.

"Watch out." I shove his shoulder without thinking.

"I know how to open a damn trailer door." He doesn't make eye contact as he fiddles with the latch.

"Really?" I place my hands on my hips and cock my head just watching him.

"Yeah, I do." He clangs the handle up and down a little harder then rips his gloves off, tossing them to the ground. "You know what, Challis? You were a cold-hearted bitch to me last night."

"Want help yet?" I don't move from my defensive stance.

"Not from you, Ms. Goody Two Shoes."

Merek screws around with the handle for thirty more seconds before he completely blows and walks away. I can't help but chuckle at the little temper tantrum he throws. He kicks up dust as he walks back to the barn and I hear several door slams.

Stepping up, I wiggle the handle counterclockwise and then lift super hard before it finally unlatches. I keep pressure pushed up against the trailer door, keeping the eager stock inside. Merek finally walks back up and nods to me. I take it as the cue to unload the calves.

The door flies open as the black calves begin jumping off in groups and run down the rest of the way of the alley. I shoo the rest of them off the trailer and shut it quickly and turn to help Merek herd the cattle down the lane.

"I need fucking help."

"Well, I'm not a shrink or a doctor to help with your crabs, so you're shit out of luck, buddy."

"Quit being a bitch."

"Damn, and swoony to top it off."

"Maverik didn't come home last night, and this group of cattle needs to go up to the far north corner of the ranch. Can you ride a horse?"

I stop dead in my tracks, and even though his sexiness has grown exponentially since I first saw him minutes ago, I want to sucker punch the fucker in the nose. "No, Merek, I don't know how to ride."

"Whatever." He stops and stares back at me. "I

know you do. Come help me move them, please."

"I have an idea, go call that skank you were making out with last night at the bar." I kick up a cloud of dust in the air and take off for the truck.

"Load up, Tori."

I jump up into the driver's seat and roar the engine to life and wait for my aunt. After she settles in her seat and buckles up, I make sure she has her money and take off. The tires blow up clouds of dirt and send small pieces of gravel sailing into the air. I hear storms of them ping off the barn and hope to hell each of them leave a dent in the pristine barn.

"Challis." The level of concern is clear in Tori's voice.

"He's a fucker and thinks I'm some dumb piece of ass who will fall to my knees for him."

"What the hell happened?"

"He wanted help trailing the cattle to the other side of the ranch and expected me just to saddle up on a pony and do it."

"Oh."

"Oh, what, Tori?" I yell, knowing that damn Merek has rattled me to the bone.

"I think you're overreacting. The man was just asking for help."

"He had the nerve to ask if I knew how to ride and then tried covering it up."

She giggles a bit before she talks again. "But did you see those abs?"

I'd never admit the fact he dampened my underwear and took my breath away to her or anyone for that matter.

"Fuck Merek Slatter."

Chapter 3

Merek

"I'll be home tonight, Marvel." I throw my bag in the back of the truck and send a nod to Maverik to hop in. "Tell Mom we'll have breakfast. I have to hit this rodeo."

"God dammit, Merek. We need to sit down and have a family meeting." Marvel throws his cowboy hat down onto the front porch.

I feel like a dick for about two seconds before I light up the tires and roar down the driveway.

"That boy is going to shoot you, Merek. You know we can't avoid this mess for the rest of our lives."

"Yeah, I know." I light up a cigarette and take a long puff. "I just need another night."

I don't miss the judgmental stare from Maverik as he looks at the burning cigarette hanging from my mouth.

"Thought you quit."

"I did."

"Really?"

"Yeah, asshole, I'm fucking stressed." I pound the dash with my fist.

"What the hell? You were with Madison last night and the hometown greeted you like a fucking hero, so what gives?"

I slam the truck to a stop at a red light and turn to Maverik. "This ranch is a fucking disaster. Dad is on the highway to hell. Marvel is going to stroke out before he hits twenty-eight, and Challis Jones has done pissed me the fuck off."

Maverik chuckles and pets the top of Jake's head.

"So, I take it that latter is the real issue with you. Get turned down by a chick and flip."

"She's a downright cold-hearted bitch."

"Are you saying that Merek Slatter has a girl crush?" Maverik holds his gut as he howls in laughter.

"You know what? Fuck off." I light up another cigarette and crank up the radio, drowning out all the outside noise and cruise down the blacktop. Pulling down my hat, I take an extra long drag from the cigarette and begin to feel the adrenaline run through my veins.

There's nothing like getting on the back of a bucker, spurring like hell, and hanging on for eight seconds. I'd give up everything just to rodeo the rest of my life. It's a scary thought to digest, but deep down, I know it's the truth. Rodeo is what makes the blood pump through my veins and the only reason I get out of bed in the morning.

It's more than being a champion. It's more of a way of life. The dusty arena, electric atmosphere, the unknown, the crowd going wild, and the thrill of winning all combined together make rodeo a strong addiction in my life.

I learned how to ride from Maverik. He was the best around for years until his little brother—me—climbed up the ranks. Then his body broke down after two major accidents where his pelvis was crushed and his shoulder was totally destroyed. He's not even supposed to ride again, but since he's the foreman of Silver Star, he has no choice but to cowboy. Rodeo has been a closed subject.

"We're here, Sleeping Beauty." I punch him in the gut.

"Fucker," he grunts as he steps up.

"Damn, you're going to need Depends before you know it, old man."

"I can still kick your ass." He reaches over and flips off my hat before I can defend myself.

"Dick."

I strategically park my truck smack dab behind the middle of the bucking chutes. It's one of my weird tendencies I always follow before a rodeo. Then from there it's all about getting hyped up. Mav has the tailgate pulled down and the red cooler popped open, fishing for one of his beers. He settles in on the tailgate next to his wingman Jake and begins scoping for a piece of ass. He usually doesn't have to try too hard. They'll all be flocking him after I ride.

Since bareback is the first event, I don't waste any time before going about my rituals. Soon the buzz of the rodeo crowd fills the air along with the other competitors prepping and others pulling in late.

A crowd of old time cowboys circle Maverik shooting the shit as I change into my riding jeans and button up my shirt. Cowboys change anywhere...well, I should say the Slatters change anywhere, not giving a shit who is around to see.

"Damn, look at the rig. Who the hell is that?" I hear Mav's voice over everyone else's.

The sound of a powerful engine purring fills the air and even grabs my attention. Looking up, I see a massive lime green Dodge Cummings packing one hell of a fancy horse trailer behind it. From the looks of it, it has living quarters and chrome from the top to the bottom. The impressive duo pulls in straight across from us and holds all of our attention.

"Not from around here. That's for sure," one of the

guys standing next to Maverik says and then shades his eyes.

The rig pulled right in front of the setting sun, making it impossible to study or to see who jumps out of it. The roar of a tractor fires up, and I know they're working the soil of the arena and I go back to focusing on my job. I drew the rankest horse that's known to buck like a son of a bitch, and I know lots of hometown people drove forty minutes here just to see me, which means the hopes of a high score.

"Mav, I'm going back." I nod to him and hoist my big black bag over my shoulder.

He waves back to me and continues on with his conversation. I don't have to remind him or tell him to follow. It's family tradition that he has my back behind the chutes whenever he's around. My friends and teammates know to back off when Maverik is around.

I settle everything out on the ground and begin strapping on my chaps and zipping up my vest. The powerful sound of hoofs beating the ground start out slow and then speed up. Soon the metal of the bucking chutes rings out in the night air as the horses are loaded in. They're feisty and thrash up against the chutes, showcasing their displeasure.

The announcer's deep voice streams from the stand above my head and the stale smell of dirt attacks all of my senses.

"Light it up, Merek." I look up to see Maverik standing before me with tape in his hand. I hold out my riding hand and let him tape it up and I dance back and forth on my tiptoes. I feel my chaps move with my dancing as I begin to roll my neck around on my shoulders, loosening up as much as possible. An

AC/DC song starts playing as they wait for the crowd to take their seats.

"Chute seven, bro, let her buck and spur the piss out of this fucker." Maverik steps up behind the chutes and I continue to loosen up and then begin stretching. I notice out of the corner of my eye that my high school douche bag rival is here but pay him no attention, acting as if I have no idea who he is.

I walk up the steps and stand on the platform behind Maverik, who is getting my horse ready. I grip onto the green metal of the shoot and begin moving side-to-side stretching out all the muscles in my legs. Then I quickly send up a prayer of safety before I hear a beautiful voice singing the National Anthem. I remove my hat out of respect and bound back and forth on my toes, staying loose and ready to roll. I'll be the third cowboy out tonight.

The crowd goes wild and the first rider is announced. I pay no attention to scores or the form of riding and instead put on my normal blinders and only focus in on my eight seconds that I have to ride to perfection.

"Did anyone come to see the two-time reigning champion of the world?"

The crowd goes wild, and it's the last thing I hear before settling down onto my horse. Once on the back of the animal and somewhat sheltered in the chute, I block everything out except for the deep voice of my brother.

"He's going to buck hard. This son of a bitch hasn't been ridden around here. He won't be a runner and will get to bucking once this gate opens. Let some hair fly."

Laying back one more time and adjusting my legs, hugging them to the barrel of the horse's body, I nod my head and the gate opens.

It's the sweetest high and quickest dose of adrenaline a guy could take. As soon as I know I'm far enough out of the gate, I spur and keep my body centered on the horse. Every bone in my body jolts and crashes together as the horse tries his damnedest to get me off of him. The buzzer goes off and my free hand comes down. The pickup men are by my side and I hop off and land feet first on the ground.

The echoing sound of the pissed off bronc pounding the dirt fills my ears as the crowd in the background roars their appreciation. I tip my hat to them and shoot them my dazzling smile as I saunter back to the bucking chutes. The back of my left hamstring is on fire, but I don't let any of my competitors see me limp. Cowboys fight like hell through pain day after day.

"Ninety-one points. Merek Slatter sitting at number one right now." The deep voice of the announcer booms out and causes the crowd to grow louder with hoots and hollers. I wave my hat one more time before disappearing behind the chutes.

I make eye contact with Mav and he knows all too well that I'm in severe pain. He throws my bag over his shoulder, nods, and leads the way back to the truck. He hoists me up on the tailgate and goes to find the medic tent.

The back of my thigh throbs as each of the muscles scream at me in pain. On the last buck, I went to spur as hard as I could and felt the rip in the back of my leg. I fumble with the lid of the cooler, trying not to move the lower half of my body. The lid goes sailing off into the air and I spot the bottle of Jack. The best pain medicine around. Twisting the top off, it only takes seconds before the dark liquid soaks my mouth and goes down easy.

I take at least two or three more shots before I spot Maverik bringing back a bag of ice and a tube of heat rub. I lay back on the bed of the truck and gaze up at the clouds when I feel Maverik adjust my leg as he tries to fix it. I listen to the crowd applaud each rider and then the announcer reads off the scores. Not one of them comes close to mine before they go to the next event.

Which means another big check for me.

"Sit up, puss." Maverik pulls my hand, dragging me forward. The pain is dulled by the combination of booze, lube, and ice.

"Doing better?" he asks with a shit-eating grin on his face.

"Pass the bottle and I'll be a bit better."

Maverik hands me the bottle and I take a few more swigs until all the pain disappears. It takes a hell of a lot more than this to get me trashed, but the perfect buzz lingers now.

After staring down at my jeans and the bag of ice my leg is propped up on, I look up and nearly pass out. A brunette goddess with piercing green eyes dressed in tight jeans and a white tank with her hair pulled up on her head stands across from me. I rub my eyes hoping to fucking hell they're playing tricks on me, but when I look again it's Challis Jones saddling up a paint horse.

It's her rig that pulled in earlier and it's her ass that now has all my senses set on fire. She's so busy working and prepping her horse she doesn't notice me flat out staring her ass down. She disappears into her tack area, and then reappears with a gorgeous etched saddle. I make out the words "National Collegiate Rookie of the Year" among the paisleys and other artwork imprinted on the saddle.

She throws the saddle up with ease on the back of her paint horse, and I don't miss her toned arms and shoulders as she works on saddling up the horse. Part of me waits for the real cowgirl to step out from the trailer, and then everything hits me like a fucking freight train. The name of her dad, her attitude, her being pissed off at my joke about her riding all sets in the little brain of mine. I've never claimed to be a genius, but everything seems to make sense right now.

Her name flies from my mouth before I think. "Challis."

Her wild brown hair flies around the top of her head as she turns to look at me. When we lock eyes, I swear I see a little smile dance on her face, but it's gone in seconds and her "I'm so not amused with you" mask cements on her face.

"You tonight?" I holler.

I watch as she walks over and stops mere feet from me.

"Naw, just thought I'd bring my pony here and try to be one of the cool kids." Her hands are firmly planted on her hips. I notice her knuckles going white from clutching them so hard.

"I see. Well, you did pick the perfect spot to try." I

draw out the word try. "To hang with the cool kids."

Just like a dark night sky on the Fourth of July, Challis explodes into a fit of fireworks.

"You asshole." She lurches forward and presses down on each of my thighs. "You have no fucking idea who I am. Just because I wasn't born with a silver spoon in my mouth doesn't mean my achievements are any less."

She pushes all of her body weight and power down into her palms, reminding me of my lingering injury, and by the look on her face she knows exactly what she's doing.

"Okay, okay, Challis, stop." I grab her forearms and lift them up but don't let go of them as I tug her into me. I spread my legs just far enough on the tailgate for her to settle in. To my surprise, she does, and it takes everything inside of me not to devour her fucking mouth. "I'm sorry."

She tilts her head in confusion.

"I said I'm sorry. Do you hear me?" I wait for a response that never comes, so I continue. "I may have come off a bit dickish the night I met you in the bar, but damn, you're smoking hot and I'm not apologizing for thinking or saying that. All the pieces just came together. I'm sorry, Challis."

"Well, you should be, Merek."

I let out a slight chuckle at her clear disapproval and cute crinkled up face. "I am, Challis, but why are you really here?"

"You asshole." She slaps my chest and jerks away from my grip, and I can't but roll into full on hysterics. She may be a tough cowgirl but easier than hell to wind up.

"Merek." I turn my head to see Madison bounding up to me. She may love the rodeo scene more than fooling around with me.

"Looks like your girlfriend is here, Champ." Challis takes a few steps back.

"She's not my girlfriend..." Before I have a chance to say another word Madison has her arms wrapped around my neck and is peppering kisses all over my cheek.

"Yeah, whatever." Challis waves me off and heads back to her trailer without another word.

Anger boils up in me, just when I finally see a sliver of hope of cracking into Challis Jones, it vanishes as soon as it appeared. Madison goes on and on about something, and I find myself still magnetized to Challis. I watch her movements as she finishes saddling her horse and wrapping his legs.

The gorgeous paint horse has no idea how lucky he is to have Challis's hands all over him.

"Merek, are you listening to me?"

"Yeah." I nod but don't look down at Madison. Soon, I hear Maverik's voice join in as he starts to entertain her.

Challis makes eye contact with her steamy green eyes and I don't look away. She turns her back and raises her tank over head. If I could walk I'd be on my feet, jogging to her and pulling her damn shirt back on. I know it's part of the rodeo lifestyle but something inside breaks, and I want to haul her sweet little ass to a room and never let her out.

She peeks over her shoulder and again I don't break my stare. If I didn't know any better I'd think she was flirting with me. I feel Madison's fingers stroke my chest, yet I'm hypnotized by Challis. She slides on a lime green button up shirt, but before pulling it all the way down I notice her starched jeans fall a bit from her hips. My heart does double time and my jeans become incredibly tight.

Her hands work flawlessly tucking in the bottom of her shirt and then she cinches her jeans back up. I can't see her hands but can tell they are busy buttoning the front of her shirt. She turns around as she does the last buttons and I'm left staring with my mouth wide open.

"Like that, Champ?" she yells.

It takes a few minutes for her words to sink in and when they finally do I'm only able to nod my head up and down. I don't miss the huge smile that covers her face before she lets down her wild hair and begins braiding it.

"Merek." I feel a hard slap on my chest and look down to Madison, who has her head propped on my good leg. "Where the hell are you?"

I glance over to my brother for some help, and he only shakes his head and lets out a light chuckle. Fucker, ain't going to be any help.

"Just checked out a bit. The pain is pretty bad." I lie a bit. I'm not checked out and the pain of my leg is bearable. It's the pain of Challis causing me the most damage right now.

My answer suffices Madison's curiosity for the time being and my gaze goes right back to the cowgirl across from me. I look back just in time to see her settle her black Stetson on top of her head. If I thought she was gorgeous in normal clothes, then holy fuck she's a goddess now.

She steps up in the stirrup and easily pulls herself up into the saddle, backs her horse up, and begins a slow walk to the warm-up pen.

"Have fun trying to fit in," I holler and tip my hat to Challis.

She doesn't respond with any words, just gives me the middle finger. The crowd around me erupts in laughter, but when I look down I see a not so pleasant look on Madison's face.

Chapter 4

Challis

I'm not the fighting type, but being interrupted by that same blonde bimbo again nearly made me want to land a punch right in her large nose. Instead, I waited for Merek's smartass comment and then flipped him the middle finger. Ever since the other night, the man has all my emotions in overdrive. Love, hate, jealousy, anger, all of them swirl around in me, but in the end all I see is his cocky beautiful ass.

I kick Teebaby into a steady trot and try to focus in on the task at hand. Winning a check and getting one step closer to taking the ranch back. I know my daddy was just blinded and looking for love, and that's how I ended up with a fucking evil stepmother. My only saving grace is there are no stepsisters, but sometimes I wish there were so this story would end up like the fairy tale. No fairy tale for this girl, just hard work and busting my ass up and down the road when possible.

Teebaby slides into a lope finding his stride and it's like he's on autopilot, his heart lives for this sport of chasing cans. If anything ever happened to him, with my daddy being gone, it would be the end of my story. He's my only other living family besides Tori. I brush those nasty thoughts away, roll my head from side to side, and begin to prepare myself mentally for the rodeo.

I catch a view of Merek hobbling up behind the chutes and settling in to watch the rodeo. Either he's desperate to see the upcoming event or very supportive of female athletes in rodeo. I secretly hope he's dying to watch me. I know it's insane and even a bit childish, but I can't help wanting to show him what I'm made of.

The help in the back starts calling names to line up, so I slow Teebaby down to let him rest a bit at a slower pace before he sees the gate, because once he sees the gate nothing will be able to stop him from gunning full speed.

The crowd lights back up after the barrels are placed out in the arena and some pumping music fills the night sky. I'm third up but can't seem to quit looking over at Merek, who hasn't been shy about staring me down. The man is about to get on my last nerve. While I'd admit part of him intrigues me, the rest flat out disgusts me.

I hear a seventeen second run and then an eighteen before it's my turn. I've never ran with these girls before, considering I'm from a different county and honestly had no idea how I'd compare.

Teebaby gets excited as I walk him over to the gate and he can see the arena lying before him and the three barrels. He's ready to run and I have to check him a couple of times by pulling back on the reins. This gets him even more excited and ready to roll. Once I know he's focused and sees the task ahead, I let him go, loosening up on the reins and settling back in my saddle for one hell of a ride.

My legs are stretched to the max as I kick him into gear. He easily turns around the first barrel taking it tight and wasting no time. I turn my head and look for number two while still kicking him on. He takes this one a bit tighter and I have to use my foot to kick it back up. I don't have time to look back to see if I kicked it too hard and sent it to the ground. Teebaby takes the third one like a champ and I send him home with my legs flying up and down encouraging him along.

I have to pull back on his reins to bring him to a stop and instantly turn back on my saddle and see all three barrels standing upright in the dirt and then the number 15:06 flash across the enormous screen. The rest is a blur as the crowd goes wild. The announcer says something about a new arena record, and I see Merek tip his hat to me.

"Teebaby, did you hear that?" I bend down, wrapping my arms around his neck and bury my face in his black mane. My hat is squished to the side and I know several eyes are on me, but I don't care.

The second thought that races through my mind is the one that I have to call my daddy to let him know of the good news. Then tears flow down into the mane of Teebaby like they have so many other times. It's still a knee-jerk reaction to want to call my dad and talk to him or share good news. It's only been four months since his death and I guess it hasn't fully sunk in.

I let the last few tears drop down into Teebaby's mane and then sit up and use the back of my hand to wipe away the rest. Everything inside of me wants to race back to the trailer, unsaddle my horse, and haul ass out of here, but I know it's not respectful, and that's the one thing my daddy made sure I was at all times. Respectful.

I sit tall on the back of Teebaby and watch the other girls run, not recognizing any of their names. Seventeens and eighteens are called out with a rare sixteen here or there. My heart swells with pride as each time is called, knowing that Teebaby and I are something special and would've set records my second year at college with no doubt.

The last cowgirl enters the arena and exits with an eighteen second run.

"Ready?" a young girl on horseback carrying the sponsor flag asks.

I nod and steady myself for the winning ride around the arena. It's the first one since my dad died and a lot fucking harder than I thought it would be. I glance over to Merek, who is still shamelessly staring. I swallow back my tears and follow the young girl on horseback.

"Let's make it a fast one," I holler to her.

"You got it, Challis."

The young girl kicks her horse into high-speed letting the sponsor flag fly high over her hat and I follow right behind her. The tears pool up and threaten to spill over as I fight to concentrate on the job at hand. My dad attended every single rodeo of mine and always watched from the bucking chute since he was the stock contractor and spent all of his time back there. He'd always watch from chute one and be there again for the victory lap. As we near the chutes, I force myself to look over at chute one and let reality sink in. The stone cold, harsh reality hit that my father is never coming back, and he loved this sport more than his own health. We pass chute one, and instinctively, I raise my right hand and offer a feeble wave. The action even shocks me and I whisper, "Bye, Daddy."

Then the tears begin to race down my cheek. The action is more painful than the day we buried him six feet under at his favorite place on his ranch. That was devastating, but this is downright soul-crushing. Life just sent me the memo that I'm on my own the rest of my life, so cowgirl up.

When I look back up, I see Merek still perched on the end of the bucking chutes, waving his hat in appreciation and whistling at me. The man really has no worry in life and I can't help but flash him a smile.

The victory lap is over as fast as it started, and even though it only lasted thirty seconds it felt like thirty days on my heart.

"Here you go. Each winner gets a bottle from our sponsor." An older cowboy hands a bottle of whiskey to me.

"Thanks."

"I knew your daddy real well. We even went to college together." The older cowboy tips his hat and looks up to me. "I mean the whole two semesters he went. Anyway, he was a good guy and would be pissing proud of ya, young lady."

This time a very weak thanks comes out as more fucking liquid pools behind my eyes. I'm not a crier or a wuss at that. I was raised by my dad and brought up like a tough little boy even though I have girl parts. It never stopped my dad from raising me with no boundaries. This crying thing has to fucking stop.

I hop off of Teebaby and loosen the cinches on his saddle, then pull his favorite treat from my pocket and give it to him. Sometimes I have to be careful he doesn't take a finger. He loves his cookies. I tuck the reins in my back pocket as I twist open the whiskey. Teebaby would follow me anywhere, so I don't worry about him spooking. I'm not a drinker, but in this moment I need to dull some pain and real freaking fast.

Hell, half the drinks people order at the bar I've never heard of and have to Google how to make the bastards. I raise the bottle, silently curse and toast my daddy, and then let the liquid flow down the back of my throat. It burns and nearly threatens me to puke, but I hold it back, not wanting to look like a pussy in front of the rodeo crowd. Weaving my way to my trailer, I take another sip and feel the immediate effects of the whiskey.

Teebaby's reins tumble to the ground from my pocket. I stop for a second and throw them over his neck and keep walking. He sticks his nose up over my shoulder and sniffs the bottle I'm holding. I can't help but giggle at my curious boy.

"No, this isn't for you. Let's get you another cookie."

He follows me the rest of the way to the trailer and I dig around in the tack pen pulling out a cookie for him. I slip off his halter and put on a new one then tie him to the trailer. Just like any other athlete, I make sure he has his food that powers all of his muscles in front of him.

A loud ruckus catches my attention, and when I look over I see Merek crashing down into the bed of his truck with that annoying blonde tumbling down onto him. The sight makes my stomach turn and an even deeper level of disgust boils up inside of me. Why does he act so damn interested in me? Clearly, he's interested in all two-legged creatures with the right parts.

I find the bottle and take another swig. This time I'm left with a spinning head and wobbly feet, but I pick up my area while Teebaby finishes his oats. The thrill of the bull riding fills the atmosphere along with its thumping music and the crowds roar of approval. This was my daddy's event. He rode through college and won Nationals but never entered the pros because of me. He was never bitter about the situation and he told me he made the sweetest lemonade with the lemons life tossed his way.

He became a stock contractor, raising and bucking the rankest bulls in the nation. It was his business and empire he was proud of and couldn't wait to pass it on down to me. It's the same business that took his life when he was gored by a bull.

The cracking sound of a gate opening throttles more and more memories of him.

"I'll go down as the guy who raised the cutest and toughest girl and bucking bulls in history. Well, not so much the cute part on the bulls."

I down more liquid as the bull riding event amps up and I can envision my daddy standing behind each bucking chute betting on his bulls to kick ass.

"Dad, are you mad you have a girl and not a boy?"
His hand reaches over and ruffles my bangs.

"Not one moment, Chally. I love you to the moon and back and always needed a mean little cowgirl in my life."

"But I don't ride bulls."

"No, you don't, and thank God for that."

It took me years growing up to get over the guilt of not being a boy and fitting into the rodeo scene with Dad. He never made me feel that way. It was all my stubbornness. It wasn't until he brought Teebaby home that I found my spot in the rodeo world.

The smell of dirt hits my senses and I can only imagine it being stirred up by the bull in the arena and some proud owner with a smile covering their face. I take another swig of whiskey and giggle when I notice the bottle is over half empty. I try to plant my elbows into the top of my thigh and miss one, nearly causing me to tumble from the side of the trailer. I steady my ass back up against the trailer and settle in, throwing my head up to the sky and asking why to anyone who will listen.

It's nearly dusk as the light clouds whirl around in the sky. My head begins to spin even faster and I feel my back sink down the side of the trailer. I slip off the ledge I was halfway sitting on and take a chug from the bottle. My ass hits the ground with a thud and I laugh out loud. Fuck, even my laugh sounds slurred.

"You okay?"

I look up into the most beautiful face I've ever seen. Unfortunately, it's attached to Merek's body.

"I's fineeee." I draw out the word fine to cover up why my speech is so slurred. I stiffen into an upright position trying to act as sober as possible.

Merek kneels down in front of me.

"Wants a drink?" I hold out the bottle to him noticing there's only about a swallow or two left.

"Challis, did you drink all of this?"

I just shrug my shoulders.

"You're going to be one hurting cowgirl in the morning."

I watch as he sets it down at his feet.

"Drink," I yell. His eyes flash between me and down to the bottle.

"What?" I try to stand on my feet. "Am I not good enough for you?"

"Challis." His hands grip my shoulders as I tumble forward.

"I just set a fucking record in that arena. Beat all

46

the hometown girls with their daddy's money behind them and you won't drink my wisskey?"

Merek has me wrapped up in one arm while he chuckles at me, which only pisses me off even further.

"Don't." I pound into his chest.

"Okay, sorry. Sorry." He bends down, snagging the bottle from the ground. "Is this what you want, Challis?" He dangles the bottle in front of my face.

"I want you to have a drink with me." I clutch the bottom of the bottle and help guide it to his lips.

"Okay, okay, calm down." He parts his lips just enough for the opening of the bottle to rest on his bottom lip, and I pour all the liquid into his mouth.

I feel him backing us up until my back smashes into the side of the trailer, and it's not until this moment that I realize I have one hand wrapped around his neck and the rest of my body pressed up against his.

"Happy now?" He crooks an eyebrow at me.

I let out a giggle.

"What's so funny, Challis?"

"You're cute, Merek Slatter."

"You're fucking wasted, Challis Jones."

I shrug my shoulders. "This is my first rodeo since my daddy died."

Tears fall down both cheeks this time as I hold nothing back nor have the willpower to hide the pain anymore.

"Come here." Merek guides my head down on his shoulder and my tears flow down the crook of his neck. I feel his hand rubbing circles on my back in a soothing motion and I don't fight any of it.

A long time passes before either of us move or

even talk to each other. I allow my body to melt into his and let him hold me as I try to calm the wild stream of tears.

"Merek." We both look up to see the blonde once again and it's as if all my senses snap right back into place.

"Go. I'm sorry." I push back on his chest. "I'm fine."

Merek takes a step back from me and I feel my body sway. My feet try to find steady ground, but none ever comes and then my body is free falling to the ground. I feel Merek's hands on me again and pulling me right back into his chest.

"Fine, uh?" He brushes a stray hair from my cheek. "I'm going to introduce you to Madison."

"No." But before I can put up more of a fight, the nosy bitch is standing feet away.

"Challis, this is Madison, and Madison, Challis. Madison and I were best friends growing up."

I listen to the bullshit flying from his mouth but don't react.

"Nice to meet you, Challis." She runs her hands down the front of her short shorts, then turns to Merek. "I'm leaving, just wanted to tell you nice ride tonight."

She steps up and places a peck on his cheek with me cuddled in his arms. I wipe at my eyes, making sure I just witnessed the scene that went down.

"You have a ride home? I know you've been drinking."

She turns and points to a tall and lean cowboy talking to Merek's brother.

"Fuck, you picked a roper out of all the cowboys around to take you home."

"Yep, see ya, Merek." She slaps him on the ass and

bounces off.

Merek turns back to me and must see the obvious stunned look on my face.

"I thought...I thought...I mean, isn't she your girlfriend?"

"No, longtime best bud and fuck buddy."

I throw my spinning head back while I let Merek still hold me up. "Good lord, I need another drink."

"You got it, cowgirl, but no more whiskey. Let's just keep this drunken state up."

"Thanks, Champ."

"I hate it when you fucking call me that."

"Good, I'll keep calling you it." I tilt my head back down and tap him on his nose.

My lips lightly brush his and he doesn't pull back. The sweet and masculine taste lingering on them intrigues me and makes me want more. This time my lips linger on his, nuzzling from side to side, then my tongue darts out absorbing his delicious taste into my mouth.

"Kiss me, Merek."

He doesn't back away and talks on my lips. "Sober Challis wouldn't like this at all."

"Sober Challis worries too much. Please kiss me, Merek."

Reservation fills his eyes, but then he clenches them shut and attacks my lips. My back is pressed up to the trailer again. Both of his large hands grab the sides of my face as he kisses me hard. I wiggle my way up to him and throw all of my body into him. After several seconds of his lips attacking mine, I play back and begin kissing him, not missing the moans of pleasure he releases in my mouth.

His taste is nothing I've experienced before and

damn near addicting. My tongue laps up every ounce of it. A few hoots and hollers fill the air and I know they're directed right at us. I remove Merek's hat and cover our two faces with it, blocking out our little make-out session.

"I see you've kissed a cowboy a time or two," he mumbles into my mouth.

"Maybe." I shrug. "Or just watch a lot of western movies."

"Which is it, Challis?"

"Shut up and kiss me, Champ."

His lips are back on mine, kissing me even harder if that's possible, as my one free hand tugs and pulls the man closer into me. Once sealed together, I trail it down the front of his shirt and search for the top of his jeans, and once I find his buckle, I flip it undone with ease.

Merek begins shaking his head side to side. "Nope, not tonight."

"C'mon." I nod toward the front of my trailer.

He grips both sides of my face and forces me to look up at him. "Challis, you're going to hate me in the morning for just kissing you."

I drop my head and mumble. "Yeah, go for the skanks anyway. I ain't no buckle bunny."

Merek doesn't respond. Instead, he hoists me up and over his shoulder, slaps my ass, and begins limping. I can tell he's in pain from the way my body sways side to side, and I feel as if I'm going to slide right off his shoulder.

"Merek, put me down now."

He doesn't listen to me, and when I look up I see the back of his pickup and feel him stop and slide me down his chest. He settles in on the tailgate of his truck and leaves me staring dumbfounded at him. He holds out a hand to me, but I don't grab it and soon feel his grip on my forearm as he tugs me into his lap, twirling me around first. I settle nicely between his legs and look around at all the staring people.

I struggle a bit to get free, or at least turn and face Merek, but he keeps my hips firmly planted.

"Here, Sis. This will help." His brother hands me a drink. "Maverik, by the way."

"Yeah, thanks. I've waited on you in the bar." I grab the drink and pound it, welcoming the burning whiskey. "Another."

He chuckles and walks away. Looking back at Merek, I'm relieved he's deep in conversation as my drunken state has begun to wear off a bit. Maverik hands me another solo cup and I slam it and then nurse the beer he hands me.

Merek's telling tales of traveling up and down the road and the different buckers he's been on. I sit and listen to him and almost feel like I'm back home with my rodeo crowd just bullshitting after a rodeo. I relax back on Merek's solid chest, laying my head on his shoulder, gazing up at the star lit night sky.

"Too much whiskey?" he whispers in my ear.

"Yeah, I'm fucked up." I reach up and lightly pet the scruff on his jawline. And even in my drunken state I know this has gone way too far already.

I remember his iced leg from earlier. "Hey, are you okay? What did you hurt?"

"I just tore some…"

My eyelids become heavy as his words slur together in my head, swirling around until my eyes finally shut and a welcoming darkness takes over.

Chapter 5

Merek

"So, you're saying we need to hire five more employees on the ranch, work these race horses, and then sell them to get securely back in the black?" I stare down my father just waiting for the answer. There's always some line of bullshit behind every single one of his adventures. The man is a gambler and a losing one at that.

"I've made a deal with Saint Johnson, and it's legit."

I slam my fists down onto the table, losing my temper and forgetting about my granddad and Mom at the table in my presence. "You've made the deal with a fucking devil and expect your boys to clean it up since you've spent all of Granddaddy's money. He worked his hands to the bone to give us this piece of paradise and you've pissed it away."

Maverik grabs me by the shoulder and forces me to sit down. "Cool it, Merek. We have no choice right now."

"And why don't we have a choice?" I glare at my father and loathe the resemblance between the two of us. "How could you do this to your own father and sons? Fuck, Mom has stuck with you through all this shit."

"Merek." My granddad's voice stops me in my tracks. I'd never think about back talking or disrespecting. "Listen and do as you're told. I'm not happy either, but the day I have to put a "For Sale" sign up is the day you'll bury me."

"Hire five good hands to work the horses. We'll

pay top dollar for their work. We'll need them for the next two months."

"Got it. We will get it done." Marvel stands to his feet, kisses our mom on the head, and heads for the door.

Always the momma's boy of the family with a heart of gold and not a wild hair on his head. Maverik rises but has other words for our father.

"When this deal is over and Granddad has his ranch back, you're leaving this place."

I watch as my mom tries to object but stops when she sees the fury cover her first born's face. "You're gone the day this ranch is out of debt and back up and running on what it was born on. No excuses. Do you hear me?"

Maverik doesn't fire up easily, but when he does no one dare fucks with him. I watch as my father nods in agreement not even putting up a fight. How horrible does life have to get to be a grown man cowering down to his son? Something doesn't settle right with me, and I have a feeling Dad is in way more trouble than just a few losing bets at the track.

"Let's go, Merek."

Each of us stops by and gives our mother a hug. I grab my granddad's arm and lead him out of the house.

"Sorry, Granddad, but someone had to do it." Maverik kicks up the dust as we walk Granddad across the dirt road to his house.

"You're right, Maverik. I'm proud of you boys and my heart just hurts for the pain—"

"Stop, we're here for you," I say as I grip on tighter to his forearm. There's one person on this planet I'll never let down, and it's him.

53

"Merek brought home a chick last night," Maverik blurts out.

"What the fuck, Mav?"

"Sorry, just trying to lighten the mood." He chuckles and tucks his hat lower on his head.

"I don't see how that's funny, Maverik. We all know he's what you young ones call a man-whore."

We both erupt into laughter at his words.

"Well, because of exactly that. He didn't bang her. He simply tucked her in and then went and slept in the hay loft with a torn hamstring."

Maverik clearly finds this fact quite comical as his laughter seems to never end, and Granddad even joins in. I guess if in all this darkness they can find some comedy it's all good.

"Now let me go." Granddad shoos my hand away. He never lets us walk him up to his house and refuses to be nursed in any fashion. The man is eighty-eight years old and still bucking hay and feeding his cattle.

We watch him walk up the sidewalk to his house, and with each step he takes it's a quaint reminder of the history this ranch holds for the family.

"Think she's up?"

"Fuck." I take my cowboy hat off and rub my head, trying to process the last few days. "I don't know, but I do know I'm going to need a fucking bulletproof vest when she realizes where she is."

Maverik erupts into another fit of laughter.

"I'm glad you get such a kick out of my life, asshole." I settle down on a bale of straw outside my little cottage.

"You're the one who got involved with her." Mav leans up against a post and crosses his arms over his chest. "But it must be serious since you broke off your fuck dates with Madison."

I use my boot to swirl around the dirt. "It's not serious. Challis hates my guts."

"Didn't look like it last night when she was mauling you."

"She was wasted and emotional. Told me it was her first rodeo since her dad passed."

"Ouch."

"I didn't push for details, but can tell it's a sore ass topic."

"Then why give up Madison? She's a sure thing."

"Because I think I want more if Challis will open up to me, and I don't need Madison in the middle of it."

Maverik lets out a long, low whistle. "Now that's a pair I wouldn't mind having in bed."

"Yeah, until they tear each other's eyeballs out." I even laugh at my own joke this time. A whinny catches my attention and I look up to see Challis's horse pacing the circle corral. I unloaded him last night and left him in the corral.

"Catch ya later, Mav, going to wake up Challis."

"I'll call 9-1-1 if I hear you screaming for dear life."

I flip him the bird and stroll up to my front door, and for the first time I feel weird entering the tiny house. Silver Star Ranch has two main houses and then a dozen small one-room homes for workers, and, well, I guess the Slatter brothers.

The house is still dead quiet and I can only assume Challis is still out. The girl is going to be hurting. Besides finishing her winning bottle of whiskey, she helped Maverik polish off a bottle of Jack, and then nursed a beer before she passed out on me and ended up dumping her beer down the legs of my jeans.

Yeah, she's going to be hurting and fucking pissed about waking up in my bed. I open the door and forget the loud creak it makes and it seems even louder in the quiet house. Challis stirs and I give her a second to wake up.

"Challis."

The sheets pool around the bed as she begins to wake up. Finally, she sits up in bed and not worried a bit that her bare breasts are exposed. The shit is not only going to hit the fan but blow clear through the fucking roof.

"Um, Challis." I point to my nipples.

She looks down and then sleepily wipes away her long brown hair from her face. Her sleep-induced face is beyond sexy with wrinkle lines imprinted in her skin. I'm sure from sleeping in one position.

"What, you've never seen tits before, Champ?"

A little humor is always a good sign, but I stay propped up in the doorjamb, staying clear from the minefield known as Challis Jones.

"Motherfucker," she mumbles as she looks under the sheets. "Did we? Did you, I mean?"

"No, but you actually begged me to."

"Ha, funny, asshole. But you promise we didn't do anything?"

"Well, I wouldn't say anything, but we didn't have sex."

"Fuck." She bounds from the bed and stumbles a bit in the tangled sheets but regains her composure. "Teebaby, my truck and trailer."

I point to the window. "It's all out there. Maverik and I took care of you."

"But how? He was getting as tanked as me."

"We called Marvel and he brought down some employees to get us all home.

She rolls her eyes. "Great, I'm glad you have employees."

"The ranch does."

"Where are my clothes? I need to go find my horse."

"Look." I point and walk closer to her. I snag a corner of the striped sheet and pull her into me and walk closer to the window. "He's out there. I fed him the rations you had in your tack pen this morning."

Her hand goes to the window with her palm pressed flat as if she's trying to pet him, and then she slowly drags it down the window. "I'm sorry about last night. I had no clue it would bring out those emotions in me."

"I quite enjoyed myself."

With her back to me, she keeps her gaze on her horse.

"I remember kissing, but that's about it. What else did we do?"

I dip my head quickly and place a light kiss on her sweet skin atop her shoulder.

"Well, you passed out when I was trying to explain how hurt I was, and then dumped the beer you were holding all over my jeans and yours."

"Clearly you talk slow and I got bored, next."

"You stripped in your truck while I was trying to seat belt you and then begged for me to take you."

"That was a bit embarrassing."

"Don't worry, I covered you up. Marvel didn't see a thing."

I feel her cringe as I speak but refuse to lie about anything from last night.

"Once we got here, you begged me a time or two to take you and then showed me how to do a somersault, and once I got you in bed you passed out again."

"How was my somersault?"

"I'd give you an eight, but would have to see you do it again in just panties to be judged accurately."

"Oh my hell. I'm such an idiot."

"Oh, and you shit your pants too."

"What?" She whirls around in my arms with panic covering her face.

"Gotcha, Challis."

My lips find hers and I place a gentle kiss on them. It's not like last night, and I'm afraid if we ever experience that passion again I won't be able to stop once started.

"What are we doing?" she asks slightly pulling, but then going back in for another quick kiss.

"Kissing."

This time she slaps my chest and steps back. "No, this and that and last night."

"Well, last night the most action I got was a cold beer covering my thigh and a part of my pecker. So, I'd say it was a friend helping another friend in need."

"I agree." She slowly nods her head up and down. "But this?"

"This can be whatever you want it to be, Challis."

"What about the blonde twat that likes to be all up in your grill?"

"Did you just go all gangsta on me?"

"No, funny business, Merek. Answer me now."

"I told her I didn't want to see her anymore. We weren't in a relationship just fuck—"

"Buddies." Challis finishes the sentences for me.

An awkward silence fills the room and I stretch out my hand to pull Challis into me, but she steps away avoiding eye contact and shakes her head.

"Talk to me," I plead.

I can visibly see her iron curtain rise up again, shielding off all her emotions and the Challis I met last night.

"I can't, Merek."

"You can't what?" I crane my neck toward her.

"I can't do this thing between us?"

"Why?" The tone of my voice is laced with anger.

"I can't."

"Fine, leave, Challis." I throw my hands up in the air and let the fury boil over. "I'm the cocky whore cowboy and it's something you don't want to waste time on."

"No, Merek." Tears begin to roll down her flushed cheeks.

I'm not sure if my anger is steaming from the family meeting or Challis turning away from me.

"I would've never been good enough for your ass anyway."

I stomp from the room, not wasting another fucking breath on the most confusing woman I've ever met in my life. I slam the front door behind me, load up my cow dog, and roar out of the driveway. Rocks spray from underneath my tires, peppering the siding of my house and I couldn't fucking care less.

Dirt Road Anthem streams through my speakers as I race up the mountainside.

Chapter 6

Challis

The house rumbles between the slamming door and gravel spraying it. I flop back down on the bed and inhale Merek's scent and let even more tears fall onto his sheets. The pain on his face killed me, and it's something I'm not proud of.

Merek Slatter is something I want after last night, but I also have the debt of thirty-two thousand weighing down on my shoulders. I stand, wiping away all the tears and remind myself there's no time for pity parties in life. I never threw one when I left college and I sure as hell won't have one now.

I slide into my jeans and smell the stench of beer. My bra is missing, which I can only conclude that the stripping stories were very real. I spot a white t-shirt draping over a drawer of Merek's dresser and snag it. Mentally, I force myself to walk through his house and not pick up on any details that may make me want Merek even more. I think about leaving him a note but don't, since it will probably only make my fuck up even worse.

My truck is parked out front still hooked to my trailer and I see Teebaby proudly trotting around the pen whinnying to the nearby horses. I shake my head at his cockiness and hope he never loses his pride.

"Sweet, baby boy," I chime as I get closer.

"You think he likes being called that?"

I turn to see Maverik, who is knee deep in mucking out a stall. I only shrug back at him, immediately feeling embarrassed by all my actions last night.

"He's a freaking badass. I'm sure he doesn't appreciate being called baby boy."

I open the latch on the pen and snag the halter on Teebaby. "Ha. Well, thanks, Maverik, he's all I got."

"See you pissed off my brother."

I shrug again. "Yeah, I did do that really good, I might add."

"He'd kill me if I told you this, but I've never seen him so concerned over one girl. He's more of the use 'em type. He even broke it off with Madison. No one has ever threatened Madison's throne."

I lead my horse out of the corral and stop before Maverik. "I just can't do this right now."

"I never thought I'd say this to a girl about Merek, but your loss, Challis. He's a damn good guy under all of his layers."

Maverik's words hit me hard. It's something Merek showed me last night.

"I see that, Maverik, but I have problems of my own I need to take care of. Not all of our daddy's set us up." I wave around with my free hand.

"You really think you know everything, don't you?"

I open the back of the trailer, hook Teebaby's lead strap onto his halter, and tie him up in his stall. Double-checking, I latch all the latches and safety pins, then walk back over to Maverik.

"All I know is I'm a cowgirl who puts one boot on at a time in the morning."

***

It's been two sleepless nights since the morning from hell. Tori has been worried and has picked up on me not sleeping. The only good news coming from it is the money. Tori handed over the calf check, and it was the hardest pill to swallow, but I accepted it. The rodeo check came in the mail and was quite hefty, plus I won a local jackpot barrel race last night.

Between that money and the wages and tips from the bar, I'm only looking at eighteen thousand dollars that I need. Which seems doable compared to thirty, but in the next minute it's a sinking ship and it's pulling my heart down.

The normal crowd fills the bar and they have the jukebox pumping out old country tunes from Johnny Cash to Merle Haggard. The music helps my shift fly by as does the growing crowd. My heart sinks when I spot Marvel and Maverik walk in and take a seat in a corner.

Without hesitation, I waltz over and take their orders as if I've never met them. They don't seem too interested in me and it actually comforts my nerves. I prep their drinks and round the bar to head back to their table, and that's when I see Merek enter.

Just the mere vision of him causes me to freeze and my hands to tremble. I set down the two drinks, then prop myself up using the sturdy oak bar. I watch each of his movements as he settles in at the table with his two brothers. All three of them resemble each other, but Merek definitely has the Hollywood factor on his side with his designer cowboy jeans and gold buckle.

He relaxes—long, lean legs in front of him—and crosses his arms. The carefree jokester isn't present tonight. Instead it's more like a pissed off cowboy arrived in its place. His jaw stays clenched, and he doesn't even attempt to take a quick view of the bar. I fucked up and hurt him. Sorry has never been my favorite word in the English vocabulary, but my daddy taught me how to use it well.

I make my way back behind the bar and snag the longneck I saw him drinking the other night at the rodeo and attach a simple sticky note to the bottom of it.

Champ,
I'm sorry. I was a bitch.
Challis

I snag a tray and place all three drinks on it and make my way over to the Slatter brothers' table. My stomach balls up with nerves as I get closer, but I fight through them and know it's the right thing to do.

"Marvel, here's your drink." I hand him his, set Maverik's down in front of him, and then wait for Merek to look up at me, but he never does, so I set his down in front of him.

I swallow my pride and put on my game face and act as if nothing is bothering me. "Let me know if you need anything else, boys."

Turning around, anger swells inside of me, and my well-known temper threatens to boil over. Everything inside of me wanted to grab Merek by the fucking ear and force him to look up at me. Yes, I was a bitch and hurt his feelings, but that doesn't give him the right to use the asshole card on me. I busy myself behind the bar washing empty glasses and stocking the ice.

The bar picks up after nine with all sorts of people from different walks of life. The Slatters have

63

remained at the corner table deep in conversation. Even the town tramps haven't dared approach them. I'm the only one who has visited their table, and that's only to give them new drinks. Maverik has waved me over a couple of times and I don't even ask. I just line up a tray of their beverages and deliver them. Merek's never asked for another beer, but I keep serving him.

I noticed Madison waltzed in about an hour ago and only nodded to Merek and joined another crowd. It instantly makes me feel like shit after leading him on the other night, him breaking off their, whatever they had, and then me running from him. My fingers strum the dark oak of the bar as I think about how in the hell I'm going to come up with eighteen thousand in the next month.

"Challis." I look up to see Maverik waving me over once again. I take my time walking over to their table since I just refilled their drinks.

"Yeah." I plant my hands on my hips.

"This is a terrible fucking idea, you guys," Merek says without making eye contact.

"We want to hire you to work at Silver Star." Maverik turns in his chair, facing me straight on.

"Excuse me?"

"Well, there's been some talk around town about you busting ass to make money—" Marvel tries to talk.

"Wait." I take a step back. "You fucking know nothing about me, and I sure as hell don't need a Slatter to save me."

"Told you she's a good hand but has a rotten fucking attitude."

"Excuse me, Merek? You have no fucking idea."

He stands straight to his feet, throwing back his chair, and begins to growl in my face. "Then fill me the fuck in, ice queen."

"Enough." I hear Tori's voice and then feel her pull me back.

"Go home, now. I'll close up." I lurch forward a couple of times toward Merek before finally giving up. By now everyone in the bar is staring at me. I untie my apron and throw it to the ground.

Tori finally leaves my side and I hear the music crank up and the endless chatter begins again in the bar. I look up to Merek and then back down to my apron with all my tips sprawled across the black material.

"I'm sorry, Challis." I look up to Marvel, who has genuinely spoken up. "We are looking for some good hands to work some colts and thought you'd be perfect. I didn't mean to offend you."

"It's fine." I kick my apron toward Merek. I go to say something but decide against it and just throw my hands up in the air and turn to leave.

"I'm leaving, Tori." I rest against the bar.

"What in the Sam hell was that? Thank God I decided to check in on you. I only stopped because the parking lot is packed."

I strum my fingers on the countertop. "I'd like to say it was their fault, but my head is so screwed up that I don't know."

Tori places her hand over mine. "You're fighting a losing battle, Challis. You need to give up the dream of ever getting your daddy's ranch back. I got this in the mail today, a copy came for me and for you. I'm guessing I got it since I'm the executrix of your dad's will."

She slides a white envelope under my hand, and when I look down I see my typed name across the front of it in a very professional font. My gut tells me it's not good news and Tori finally saying the words to deflate any hope I had originally had.

"Thanks." I take the envelope from her and walk away from the bar. Before exiting the bar, I send one last glance over to Merek, who is now being entertained by Madison.

My truck is parked under the streetlight. Going home to an empty house and reading this depressing letter doesn't sound like fun at all. I pull down my tailgate and hop up on it. I stare at the envelope for several minutes before opening it.

Challis Jones,

This is the last letter you'll be receiving on behalf of Mrs. Cody Jones. The ranch currently owned by her in Fulton County will be sold in forty days unless the full thirty-two thousand owed against it is paid in full to her. In addition, the full shares of savings, stocks, and bonds in Cody and Challis's names are to be signed over to her.

Please be advised this will be your final notice.
Sincerely,
Harrison Clemens
Attorney

I wad the letter up and toss it into the parking lot. "More demands from the bitch. Every. Single. Damn. Time. She adds to her demands."

My words are lost in the night air. That evil snake named Lola came into my life my senior year and has done nothing but leech her way into my daddy's account. I fucking swear the monster danced on my daddy's grave when he was finally buried. He always wanted a woman in his life and dated so many women while I was growing up but landed quite the humdinger.

She's done nothing but fight to sell the ranch since the day he died, and it looks like in forty fucking days she'll have her way. Daddy had a couple of clauses in his will preventing her from selling it the day he died. He was always a smart businessman, but how in the loving hell he thought I could ever fork over thousands to save it is beyond me.

His death wasn't planned, and I know he had all sorts of money tied up in expanding his stock and traveling further west with his bucking bulls. The worst part of this story is that Lola would rather drain the tied up bank accounts than keep the ranch, and in all honesty the bank accounts are worth more than the stupid ranch, but it's my history, pride, and roots that I want.

I pound my fists down into the tailgate and feel my anger spew over in the form of tears. And this time I don't try to hold them back. The last flicker of hope I had is blown out with the letter.

"This is bullshit."

I look up in the dark parking lot to see the outline of Merek holding the letter. I don't even have the steam to comment back.

"What is this, Challis?" He steps up into the light, closing the distance between us.

"You know how to read."

"Quit being a fucking bitch." He waves the paper in front of my face. "I didn't do this to you."

"Nope, you sure didn't."

"So, what in the hell is going on?"

"Nothing for a carefree champ like you to worry about."

His hand grabs my chin and forces me to look at him. "My dad has lost everything at the fucking horse races and put my granddad's ranch into the red. He's fucked over the wrong people with big money. So, don't you ever throw that in my face again."

I rip my face from his hold. "Want to know, Merek?"

He steps back, crosses his arms, and waits. It's like the standoff that's built up between us is about to go down with neither of us backing down. I slide off the tailgate and walk right up to him.

"My daddy died about four months ago. Gored to death by one of his prized bucking bulls that I told him to sell a long time ago, but it was good bucker and all the talk in the circuit."

"Elvis," he whispers.

"Yep, Elvis was more fucking important to my daddy than his common sense or even his health. But wait, let me back up a few years. He married Lola the summer after my senior year, and she's a royal cunt, but I bit my tongue since she seemed to make my daddy happy. Well, guess what, he's dead now and Lola wants money and a lot of it."

"This." He holds up the crumpled letter.

"That. I've already drained all my accounts with just my name on them and paid her over two hundred thousand dollars. Sold my calves, the bucking bulls I owned with my dad, my extra saddles, tack, right down to the underwear I'm wearing. I kept Teebaby, my truck, and trailer in hopes of making some more money this summer."

Breathless and on the edge of hyperventilating, I bend over and rest my palms on my knees and try to cool down. "My three months just went to forty fucking days, and I have nothing now."

"How much do you still need to pay?"

"Eighteen thousand and sign over all my daddy's accounts, which are fucking worth nearly one point two million." I throw my hands up in the air. "Her newest and latest demand. It's like she just keeps taunting me since she knows I'll never make it."

"Then why is she dicking with you paying her eighteen thousand."

I stand straight up and cover my chest. "Because it's her last fucking dagger to my heart, tormenting me with the fact I can never go back home to the one place I love the most in this world. The one place where all my memories are and the soil that my daddy is buried in."

"I've got that money, Challis."

Those five words cause me to lose my shit.

"No, Merek. No," I scream and back up.

"I've got it. You can be as bullheaded as you like, Challis."

"Stop." Tears begin streaming down my face. "I wasn't raised to be a victim."

I take another step back and trip over something, falling to the ground and let out a twisted giggle between the tears, considering I've hit rock bottom finally. Picture-perfect, in the parking lot of a bar with Merek Slatter witness to it all.

"Calm down." I feel my arms being lifted and then my body pressed against Merek's.

"I just want to forget it all, Merek, all of it. Why can't I just move on? Go down the road and rodeo, leaving behind everything."

He leans back, grips my face, and begins brushing away my tears. "Because it's your roots and you never leave those. We have wild hearts, but always know where home is."

"So, I just die trying and get my heart broken in the end?"

"The way I see it, you have two choices, Challis. Take my money, or come work for us on the ranch and we can hit as many rodeos together as possible."

"Well, I'm not taking your fucking money, Champ."

"Then it looks like I just hired your ass."

I bury my face in his chest and shake my head. "God, my life. I would've bet my left nut I'd never be in this predicament."

Merek laughs hardily into the top of my hair. "Let's get out of here."

"To where?"

Chapter 7

Merek

Challis stays glued to the passenger door and stares out her window as I drive us to my favorite spot on the ranch. We already made one stop picking up a piping hot pepperoni pizza, a case of beer, and some girly junk food.

"Ever wonder if we are all just destined to be fucked over?" Her voice is low and full of defeat.

"Every time before I climb on the back of a bucker, but it's the chance I take and then relish in the afterglow when I kick life's ass."

"I think you missed your calling in life, Merek."

I look over at her and finally make eye contact. I hold my hand out and have to hold myself together when she places her hand in mine. "What's that?"

"Writing self-help books. You're pretty inspirational." She stops and clutches my hand. "Why are you being so nice to me right now?"

"Because you bought my beers tonight and put a cute little apology note on one of them. A heart and *xoxo* would have sweetened the deal. Just saying."

I lie like a rotten bastard, because the truth is something I can't even comprehend. And it goes a little like this…the moment I came into contact with her green eyes she captured me. I fell like a brick for the free-spirited cowgirl and know I'll never get enough of her. She definitely did something to my lonely heart and is going to devastate me, but it's the only storm I want to be in.

Her giggles fill the cab of my truck. "I'm serious, girl, next I expect hearts and flowers."

71

"Isn't that what the girl is supposed to want?"

"Yeah, but I have a feeling you're going to crush me in the end, and I just want to enjoy the ride."

This time I cringe at the honest words that flow from my lips. And I'm relieved when Challis doesn't respond and only flops her head back on the headrest. We ride the remainder of the way in silence. I'm lost in the tornado of everything Challis Jones and wish she wasn't such a stubborn jackass. It would be nothing for me to fork over the money, and I'd do it in a heartbeat with no strings attached. Seeing her broken down the other night after her run at the rodeo and then again tonight in the parking lot killed me.

I'd do it just for her to be able to go home and live out her own fairy tale on her daddy's ranch. With the shit storm going down on Silver Star, I understand how real the threat can be and how I'd go to the ends of the earth to save it for my granddad.

"We're here." I put the truck into park and hop out.

"And here is exactly where?"

"My favorite place on Silver Star."

"Wow." Challis's jaw drops when she looks out the front window.

We are on the back of the property we call Slatter lot. It's an expansive pasture with rolling hills and a large pond in the center of it. Granddad built us boys a fort and hung a swing under a large willow tree that sits atop a rolling hill facing the pond. And tonight the moon lights up the pond with thousands of stars decorating the pitch-black sky.

"Pretty cool, uh?"

"It's gorgeous, Champ." I watch as Challis stares

straight ahead to the pond and clambers to find the handle.

I snag the pizza, beer, and junk food from the back seat and hop out.

"Challis, there's a blanket under the back seat. Grab it."

She rounds the front of the truck with the blanket in her hand. "How many girls have you done on this?"

"None." I can't help but laugh.

"Liar."

"I'm not lying. But I'd like to nail one girl on it." I send her a quick wink and lay the blanket out.

We settle in on our own sides of the blanket, digging into the pizza and both of us throwing back our fair share of beer.

"Do you ever swim in that?"

"Yeah, when I was younger."

"Why not now?"

"To be honest, I'm not home that often. This is the longest in years."

"Why home now?"

"Taking a break and trying to be here for the family."

"Hey." Challis scoots over, placing a hand on my upper thigh. "I'm sorry about your ranch problems and being such a judgy pants."

I just nod, not even wanting to think about the mess my father has us in.

"I'll take the job, but the pay better be good, and I'll need to travel to as many rodeos as possible."

"That a girl."

"I'm not going to give up, Merek. There's no doubt I'll probably lose this war with Lola, but I'd never forgive myself if I gave up now."

I lean over and place a light kiss on her forehead.

"Only one stipulation, Challis."

Her defenses go straight back up. "You take me as your traveling partner to your rodeos."

"Won't I cramp your style?"

"Yes, but I'll enter up with you."

"Why?"

"Because I want to."

"Want to what?" Challis leans in closer.

"Rodeo with you."

"But why?" she asks, leaning in so close her breath tickles the skin on my jaw.

"I want to be with you."

"Good answer, Champ." She reaches up and places a light kiss on my cheek.

"God, I hate that nickname." I surprise her by flipping her onto her back and covering her body. "But it's so sweet coming from your lips."

"What are we doing, Merek? If it hasn't been made clear, I'm not so good at this type of stuff." She gestures between the two of us with her hands.

"We are saving our roots, going to work our asses off, rodeo together, and see where this takes us."

"Kay."

"Are you good with that, Challis?"

"I think I can give it a try, but you have to understand, I'm a fucking mess."

"Two train wrecks about to collide together." I smile down at her.

I feel her arms wrap around the back of my neck and tug me down closer to her.

"Shut up and kiss me."

"This seems to be your favorite line."

My lips find hers and relish in the sensation again.

Her taste is something I never want to forget. I waste no time darting my tongue into her mouth, and Challis welcomes me and kisses me back just as hard and fast. I feel her hands ripping at my shirt, tearing it away from my chest. Then her nimble fingers fumble with the button of my jeans, and I do her a favor by raising up a bit allowing her to unbutton them.

I plant my elbows on the blanket and cradle her head, cementing her lips closer to mine. Desire courses through my veins and once this starts I'm afraid I'll never be able to stop. She rubs her palms up and down my back and then goes back to my fly, coaxing me to kiss her harder. Her tender touch sends my senses spinning and brings out a carnal desire in me.

I pull away from her lips. "Challis, you need to slow down."

"Why?" She offers up a pouty face.

"I'm not going to be able to stop if you keep pushing me."

She slowly raises her head and roams her lips over the tender skin on my neck and then darts out her tongue leaving a wet trail along my skin. Her hands go back to my zipper and dart under my boxers this time. Her actions cause me to gasp out loud.

I hear my cellphone go off in the cab of the truck and ignore it as I pull Challis's shirt up over her head, leaving her exposed only in a bra. Slowly, I pull one perked nipple from underneath the lace of her bra and dip my head. My tongue swirls around the peaked flesh, and this time it's Challis moaning and bucking underneath me. The sounds of her pleasure send me into overdrive. My teeth sink into her nipple as my hand wanders down to her zipper. My phone goes off several more times.

"You better go answer that," Challis says breathlessly.

I growl around her nipple, but deep down, agree with her.

"Don't move a muscle."

I race to the truck and see Maverik's number scrolling across the screen.

"Somebody or something better be on fire," I growl into the phone.

"It's Granddad. They rushed him to the hospital."

My world stops as all the blood drains from my face.

"I'm coming, Mav."

I end the call and toss the cell across the dash.

"Challis."

"I'm here. Let's go."

"Challis."

"Breathe, Merek, breathe. Get in the truck."

She tucks me into the passenger seat, rounds the corner to the driver's seat, and hauls ass.

Chapter 8

Challis

The moment Merek stands up, the night chill covers my body. I hear him answer the phone just feet away from the blanket, and then Maverik's words slice through the night air. I toss on my shirt and go to Merek.

"He can't…"

"Merek, he won't. Stop."

I drive back out of the pasture trying to remember all the turns and different dirt roads Merek took. He's in no condition to ask. He's gone completely pale and frozen with fear. Just from the bit of conversation we've had I know his granddad is his favorite person in the world. In this moment, I know how he feels. I remember the night I rushed to the ER for my dad.

Finally, I hit pavement and recognize my surroundings on highway twenty-six. I waste no time or horsepower as I race to town. We pull into the lit up driveway of the hospital. Slamming the truck into park, I let out a sigh of relief. Merek is out of the truck, grabs my hand, and pulls me all the way across his bench seat. He jogs into the hospital, towing me behind. Hand in hand, we round the corner and come face to face with the Slatters sitting in the waiting room.

"What happened?" Merek is breathless and his voice sounds terrified. I use my free arm to run it up and down his forearm in hopes to provide some comfort to him.

"They're thinking another mild heart attack." Marvel is the only one to reply.

"Where is he?"

"You can't see him right now, Merek, they're trying to stabilize him." Marvel stands up.

I feel Merek's knees buckle and wait for him to hit the ground. I lead him over to the nearest chair and force him to sit, but when he refuses to I push harder until he sits. He grabs my hand and drags me down into his lap.

"Be my shield," he whispers into my ear.

I wrap my arms around his neck and rest my head in the crook of his neck as we wait. My eyes drift shut and soon I pass out in his arms.

"Merek."

I feel my body shake.

"Merek, your granddad would like to see you."

I sit up straight and come face to face with a nurse and a stirring Merek underneath me.

"Excuse me," he mumbles.

"Your granddad is just fine and would like to see you."

I stand up and stretch out my sore muscles from the odd sleeping position. I feel even worse when I see the stiff cowboy try to stand up. He rubs out his leg and I feel like shit knowing I slept pressed to him and his injury.

"I'll be back." He stops in front of me and kisses my forehead.

"I'll be here, Champ." I send him a little wink before collapsing back down into the overstuffed chair.

I look over to Maverik, who sends me an approving nod. He seems to be the boss of the crew, so it eases my nerves a bit to know I have somewhat of an approval from him.

"Do you need anything, Challis?" Marvel asks.

"No, thank you. I'm fine."

"Are you my son's flavor of the month while he's home?" An older version of Merek speaks up. "He must've got caught with his pants down and didn't have time to take you home. God knows he'd drop everything for my dad."

"Enough." The woman sitting next to him slaps his forearm.

"Like Merek treats her any better."

"He does." The two words fly out of my mouth before I have the chance to slap my palm over it.

"Dad, you might want to show her some respect. We just hired her to help out with the colts." Maverik stands to his feet.

"Do you even know how to ride?"

Now the man has me seeing red and I'm ready to tear his throat out, but before I have a chance to respond to the asshole, Maverik does.

"You bet your ass she does. She set a new record down in Newton and she's the daughter of Cody Jones, so you might want to shut your foul mouth before we are one hand down."

"It's fine. I'll wait outside. I'd say it was nice meeting you, but it wasn't."

I turn and leave before I hear any further stupidity and hatred fall from the man's mouth. As I walk out, I do hear 'that's Tori's niece.'

I make my way outside and think I should text Merek. Well, yeah, a novel thought if I had his number. I pull my phone out of my pocket and see several missed calls and texts from Tori. Yeah, my actions were a bit selfish.

Me: I'm fine. With Merek- his granddad got put in the hospital.

Tori: Need a ride?

Me: I'd like to wait for Merek.

Tori: I was so damn worried about you. Are you sure you're okay?

Me: Fine and actually not giving up the fight. Slatters hired me to train some colts and I'm going to do local rodeos with Merek.

Tori: I love you, but I just don't want to see you get your heart broken over all this.

Me: I know ☹

Tori: And I'm not talking about Merek.

"You okay?" The deep voice of Maverik startles me, causing me to toss my phone into the bushes.

"Jesus." I clutch my chest and listen to his deep chuckle. He bends over and snags my phone for me. "Well, not now, I just shit my chaps."

"My dad is a dick."

"I see that."

"He and Merek have never seen eye to eye. It's always been Merek and Granddad. Then Marvel and Mom. I'm the loner."

I shrug. "It's fine, really. I've been around my fair share of asses in my life."

"Well, it's not fine, and I hope it doesn't make you change your mind about the job offer."

"Nope, already told Merek I'd take it, plus I need the money really bad."

Maverik nods to me and then we both hear the whooshing of the doors opening behind us.

"He's going to be okay. It was only a scare and they're adjusting his meds. He just wanted an update on hires." Merek pauses for a moment. "Why are you two out here?"

"Dad," Maverik blurts out.

"I just needed fresh air."

"That son of a bitch." Merek's hand is on the door, but I get to him before he rips it open.

"It's not worth it." I tug on him. "Take me home, so I can shower and get ready for my first day on the job."

"I'm so sorry, babe."

"It's fine. Really. Tensions are high with everyone, but please take me home or actually to the bar, so I can get my truck and we can start working the colts."

"Got it." Merek grabs my hand. "I'll see you back at the ranch in twenty, Mav."

"See ya two." We both watch as he heads back into the hospital.

"Was my dad that bad?"

"Well, not the friendliest of people I've ever met."

"What did he say?"

I ignore his question, round the front of his truck, crawl in through the driver's door, and settle in the middle.

"Challis."

He roars the engine to life but doesn't move. Instead, he stares me down.

"Basically that you're a man-whore and I'm just the flavor of the month."

"He didn't."

"Don't." I grab his wrist, stopping him from vaulting from the cab. "Let's both focus on the tasks ahead of us and not let the evil people in our life ruin it for us. It's a waste, Merek."

"How dare that dickhead talk to you like that?"

"Who cares? I've been raised around asshole cowboys my whole life. Water off my back, and I'd settle being your flavor of the month if that means I get one month with you."

Now that gets his attention, Merek quizzically stares down at me. "Did you just admit that you're into me even a little bit?"

"Maybe." I shrug.

"Shut up and kiss me, Challis."

I giggle when I hear him use my line on me, but do what I'm told and kiss his perfect lips.

Chapter 9

Merek

"What a last twenty-four hours." I slam down my shovel.

"You can say that again, little brother."

"You guys, I don't know what I'll do the time Granddad doesn't come home from the hospital. I don't know that I'll survive it."

"You will, because you have us," Marvel says.

"I still can't believe the shit storm Dad has us in. I mean, who in the hell can blow nearly a quarter of a million betting on the horse races and be fucking dealing with Saint?"

"Merek, I think this has been a long time coming with Dad. He's blown everything and now we are here to pick up his mess."

"The colts that Saint's hired hand dropped off are gorgeous," Marvel adds.

"Yeah, probably bought with drug money," I add as I tip back my longneck.

I can't fucking stand the man, and everyone in the great state of Texas knows he's a fucking criminal and has basically fucked over every large rancher at some point in time. He's the pimp of the land and no one crosses him, except for my greedy ass dad who's gone into debt with the rotten son of a bitch. I'll be damned if I'll let my dad put Granddad's ranch up for collateral. I'd rather work for the fucking devil himself.

"I still can't believe this shit we're knee deep in." Maverik pops open a longneck and takes a seat on a straw bale.

"Me either, but we need to keep the details from Mom." My eyes shoot to Marvel's. "She thinks Dad's been just dabbling in the races, but he actually lost all the money on a couple lots of fat cattle."

"Again, how in the hell are we going to survive this shit storm?" I ask.

"That's how you're going to get through it while we both nurse a cold beer." Maverik points his finger.

When I look up I see Challis walking toward us in tight as hell and sexy as sin blue jeans, a white tank, and a blinged out ball cap. Pieces of her wild hair dance out the back, but it's her tits that hold my attention.

"Hey, boys."

I drop my gaze down to her boots not to be rude, and the damn designer boots of hers even turn me on. *What in the fuck was I thinking hiring her on?* If I'm popping a boner just watching her walk into the damn barn, what will I do when she's on horseback?

"Merek." She waves a hand in front of my face. "This is where you say 'Hello, Challis.'"

I snag her hand and drag her into my lap, shove up my cowboy hat a few inches, and give her a proper hello with my mouth and tongue. I take a few seconds to really enjoy her sweet lips before I pull back.

"Or I'll take that as a hello." She taps on my nose and bounces up from my lap. "But I'm here to work and won't be just eye candy. Marvel lead the way."

Marvel jumps from the straw bale and walks out into the pasture with Challis chattering away.

"That shit's good for him," Maverik says.

"Sure is." I agree.

"And I think it's best you two aren't working side

by side."

"No shit. I might die of an erection or go blind at the bare minimum."

"I'm going to head into town and order enough grain for these colts and pick up some other supplies."

"Sounds good, I'll get to work on fixing the motor on the exercise machine, and I guess those two," I point to Challis and Marvel standing out in the pasture, "they'll create the plan of attack on how we are going to get these thirty colts broke and in shape in three months."

I give Maverik a brother slap-hug combo on the back before walking off and can't help but take one more peek over my shoulder at Challis. It was a massive mistake, because I catch a glimpse of her just as she climbs up on my favorite childhood horse and trots off. The damn girl is going to break my dick if we don't get some alone time real quick!

***

"Everything is set for tomorrow. Colts are lined up to start training, equipment is running, and all hired hands have checked in today." Marvel's on the phone with Satan himself. It kills me that my fucking father has put our baby brother in this position. Marvel's always been the business savvy one out of us brothers and loves the ranch life. He doesn't have any of the rodeo blood pumping through his veins like Mav and I do.

After several minutes, he ends the call and offers all of us a weak smile. "Everyone, listen up."

All the hired hands keep chattering at a low level and don't pay one ounce of respect to Marvel. I watch as he tries to continue talking and wait for the man to stop mid-sentence and rip into their asses for being disrespectful pukes. I glance around for Challis and don't see her.

I nod to Maverik and as if he seems to know what I'm looking for, he points to the front entrance of the barn where Challis is on her phone and kicking some gravel up as she talks.

"Listen up." My voice booms through the barn. "You are here to do a job and when your boss is speaking I suggest that you listen up or you'll be hitting the road."

It takes everything inside of me not to drop the F bomb a time or two but know that would floor Marvel. He's all business and the utmost professional when dealing with employees.

And like magic the ignorant assholes shut the fuck up while Marvel goes on. "Every morning you're to be here at six a.m. We will have a nutrition team who will feed and water the horses, while others of you will be mucking out the stalls and putting down fresh bedding. We've selected three of our best riders to spend their day training colts. Any problems come to me. No questions asked. If we don't get this job finished then no one gets paid. See you in the morning."

The group quietly disperses in all different directions. Some going to their home for the night while others are staying in the bunkhouses since we brought some in from out of state.

"Nice speech, little bro." I pat Marvel on the back, proud as hell of him.

"Thanks." He shrugs and collapses on a straw bale.

"You wear your fucking heart on your sleeve."

Maverik steps up to him. "Tuck that bitch in your back pocket and make this happen."

"You've got this, Marvel, and we'll be here every step of the way," I add.

"Until the circuit starts back up and you hit the road, Merek. I've been doing this shit the last two years. Little fucking stunts like this to pull Dad out of debt. Do you know how fucking tired I am? And out of all the brothers, I'm ready to quit."

His words shock me. I know he's been working his ass off here on the ranch but had no idea that Dad had him tied up in other shit.

"What are you talking about?" I finally ask.

"Enough." A deep familiar voice comes from the entryway of the barn.

We all look up to see Granddad walking toward us. He's using his cane today and that's not a good sign at all. I'd offer to help him to a seat but know he'd whop me upside the head with that cane and then threaten to stick it up my ass. He may be old as dirt but still wakes up every morning, feeds some cattle, and is always dressed in his Wranglers, button up shirt, and ol' straw hat.

We all wait for him to settle in on the straw bale and none of us dare question him. We've all had our fair share of ass whippings with the willow branches at his hands, and I'll admit it was all well-deserved whippings.

"We are going to make it through this, boys, and when we do, your dad is being removed from the business permanently. It breaks my heart to do this. I made the decision the other night I was admitted to the hospital." He pauses for a moment as his voice cracks. "He's my blood, my only son, and this isn't easy, but I will not have his addiction ruin the empire I built for you three. Once Silver Star is back into the black I'm putting all of it into all of your names. So, enough fighting. Figure it out, boys."

We all sit in silence. I'm stunned shit has gotten so bad for him to kick our dad out of the business. Silver Star has always been Granddad's. He's claimed that he's been waiting for the perfect time to pass it on, and I guess this is it.

"But we just can't…"

"Merek, let go of the damn past before it eats you alive," Granddad scolds.

I digest each of his words, realizing how true they are. The sound of footsteps distracts all of us, and when I look up from dirty boots I see Challis entering the barn.

"Am I interrupting?" she asks with her green eyes widening.

I can't help but smile back at her innocent beauty. She's been on horseback all day, mucking out stalls, and everything else she's been asked and looks like Miss America to me with her olive skin, dangerous green eyes, and wild brown hair flying everywhere. I force my gaze to stay away from her tits with Granddad sitting in front of me.

"No, miss, I'm just leaving." Granddad hoists himself up off the straw bale and Challis immediately grabs his elbow helping steady him. I cringe as she tries to help the stubborn old fart.

"Well, thank you, sweetie." He looks up to her and smiles. My jaw drops in shock as I look over to my brothers—they seem to be having the same reaction.

"I'm Challis Jones. I will be working here for a few months."

"I'm Marve Slatter, or as most call me, Granddad."

"Oh." She covers her mouth and then she looks at me. Granddad doesn't miss any of her reactions.

"You must be the young beauty Merek's been talking about."

She shrugs her shoulders and blushes, and I cross my arms, lean back on the post, and watch this scene play out.

"Well, no disrespect, sir, but Merek does talk a lot of shit."

Granddad's deep chuckle fills the barn. "That he does, but I've heard enough about this green-eyed beauty who's turned him down too many times to count and is the only thing he can think about."

"Okay, okay." I push off the post. "Enough talking, you two."

"No, really, tell me more." Challis hooks her arm in his elbow. "May I walk with you?"

"Why yes. To that white house over there, please."

"What the hell?" Maverik tosses his hat into the dirt. "You'd beat our ass if we tried to help your crippled ass."

Granddad turns back to us three. "If I've taught you three boys anything it's that you never let a pretty little lady escape."

I don't miss the quiet stare from him and know from those simple words he's telling me so much more.

We watch as the duo walk away toward his house, and every once in a while I see Challis throw her head back in laughter and can almost bet on the stories that he's telling her.

"I'm going to marry that girl."

The words drift around in the barn, and I watch as

both of my brothers' jaws drop.

"You've known her a whole whopping two weeks, and most of the time you two have wanted to kill each other," Maverik says.

"Don't you have to be boyfriend and girlfriend first?" Marvel asks.

"Two wild hearts have crashed together, boys, and I'm going to make her mine. Just watch me." I pat them both on the back and walk out into the Texas sun feeling happier than I've ever felt. Even with the stress stemming from our ranch and the threat of Challis losing hers, life has never felt sweeter.

I take long strides across the gravel road to meet Challis as she bounds back down Granddad's sidewalk and catch her before she hits the dirt road. I pull her in with both arms and then grip the back of her head.

"You make me happy, Verde."

"Verde?" She wrinkles her nose at me.

"Your nickname from me."

"Care to explain?" She rubs her nose into mine.

"Your green eyes are fucking gorgeous and are the first thing that attracted me to you, and Verde is green in Spanish."

"Wow, you're so deep, Champ."

"Shut up and kiss me."

And like a well-oiled machine, our lips seal together and melt into a kiss. I nudge her back until her ass hits the top of the fence lining the property. She sinks her tongue deep into my mouth, nearly causing me to rip off all of her clothes, but then her phone goes off.

"Sorry." She pushes back off my chest. "It's Tori."

I have to take two steps back, shoving my hands

through my hair trying to tamp down my fucking raging hormones.

"I have to go work at the bar tonight." She steps up to me and winds her arms around the back of my neck and jumps up into me. Her actions surprise me, but I'm quick enough to catch her ass in my hands.

"Not if I kidnap your ass."

"Merek, I have to, just for tonight, to give Tori the night to train the new help. She was nice enough to let me go to give this a try."

"Are you talking us or riding ponies?"

She takes a moment to respond. "Well, both I guess."

"Want me to drive you in?"

"Naw, I got the green beast over there, but you could come in for a drink or two." She drags her tongue along the seam of my lips.

"You better stop, or I'll march your ass right over there to my house and take you."

She waggles her eyebrows at me. "Tonight, Champ, you can have all of me.

Chapter 10

Challis

A goofy ass grin covers my face all night as I pour cold beer and mix up cocktails, but I can't help it. I've tried to wipe it off a time or two and plaster on a poker face, but it just keeps creeping right back on. I know it's a mixture of the way Merek makes me feel alive again and the sliver of hope that I just might pull off getting the ranch back forever.

I can't help but picture Lola's face as I hand over the check and sign the final papers. I know I'm stooping down to her evil ways, but a girl can only hope.

"Coors, please."

I look up to see a familiar face sitting on the other side of the bar, and he must pick up on my confusion of trying to place him.

"Preston. Met you out at Silver Star today. We'll be working together the next three months."

"Oh, yeah, sorry. It's been quite the day, and, honestly, I'm exhausted."

"Me too, and you're still working."

"Yeah, just for a couple more hours." I push over his frosty mug. "Want a tab?"

He relaxes back on the barstool and shoots me a sly grin. "Yeah, I think I do."

"You got it."

"So, how did you get hooked up with Silver Star Ranch?" he asks.

I keep filling orders and try my best to keep up in conversation with the chatty man. "I know the Slatter

92

boys from serving them in here."

Preston is quite the charmer with his golden blond hair and very, very thick accent. His skin is olive, and, well, his damn muscles speak for themselves, bulging from his white t-shirt.

"I see. I just moved in from Oklahoma and live to ride. So you can say I landed the perfect gig."

"Awesome. Nice chatting. I have to go work the floor now."

I sneak away from the bar before the chatty man can ask another question. I'd love to tell him I'm with Merek, but am I? What do I say…well, I'm lined up to screw a Slatter tonight, so I'm taken? I mean, most women simply say 'I have a boyfriend'. But that's something I've never really had. When I start to think of all the logistics, my giddy smile vanishes and my mind is bogged down.

Thank God this job is pretty much robotic in the fact I could do it with my eyes closed. I take orders, fill orders, clean tables, and then repeat the steps. Every single time I step behind the bar, Preston has a question or some funny comment, and even as annoying as he may be, at least he's keeping me company.

I check my phone and then remember I don't have Merek's number, and he doesn't have mine yet. Probably a good indicator that we both suck at the boyfriend/girlfriend thing. Then my mind takes a wild ride thinking about all the women he's been with, and I wonder for the first time if he's ever been in a serious relationship at all, or even for that fact been with one woman over a long period of time. The only good thing coming from checking my phone is the fact there's one hour until last call.

"Hey, little lady, you look a little lonely." Arms wrap around my midsection as a breath tickles the flesh of my neck. I crane my neck to see Merek's gorgeous face all up in my business.

"Hey, you can't be back here." I whirl around in his arms.

"What they going to do, fire you, Verde?"

"That name is dumb. You can do better." I roll my eyes.

Merek dips down, kissing the tip of my nose. "What was so damn intriguing on your phone?"

I plant a kiss on his lips before talking. "I was going to text your ass but then realized I don't have your number, and then I started wondering about stuff."

"What kind of stuff?" He tilts his head in a genuine fashion.

"Like about your past and girlfriends and if you've been loyal to a woman." I chose to lay it all out on the line for him and wait for his reaction.

"If I answer no is this over between us?"

"If you lie then it's over between us."

"Then no, I've never had a real girlfriend or been loyal to any girl for that matter."

The fear covering his face as he is honest with me actually melts my cold heart a bit.

"Thanks." I kiss him quickly, biting down on his bottom lip and then spin him around and slap his ass. "Out, I have to work. I'll bring you a drink in a bit."

He rounds the bar and rests on the end of it watching me work and I try like hell to pretend I don't see him. After a few moments go by I give up and turn to him. "What?"

"So, you're not mad at me?"

"For?" I raise my eyebrows.

"Being honest with you."

"Actually, I'm not. I'm relieved, because I suck at relationships and apparently you do too, so we might just work out."

I watch all of his muscles relax as he walks over to a table to join his brothers. I'm used to waiting on Maverik and Marvel, but having Merek join is something new. Watching the three of them come together to save their granddad's ranch and essentially their heritage, gives me hope there's good in this crazy ass world.

"Hey, cutie, I'll take another cold one."

I look up to catch the beer Preston sends sailing my way across the bar just in time before the mug sails over the bar onto the floor.

"Whoa. My name is Challis, and I don't expect to be called anything else."

He holds his hands up in a defensive posture. "Sorry, just thought since Merek was friendly we all could be."

"Excuse me?" I take a step closer to him and point my finger at his nose. "You have no fucking right to treat me any way. I'd kick you out right now, but seeing that we have to work together the next three months, I'll let it go this time."

Using too much force, I flip back the Coors handle and let the beer flow into a new frosty mug. The desire to spit in his beer is overwhelming, but I fight it when I hear someone call my name.

"Challis, I'm dying of thirst over here."

I look up to Merek, who has his arms raised up holding his cowboy hat. I just flash him a grin and then feel the cold amber liquid run onto my hand. I hand Preston his beer and don't exchange a word with him before heading off to grab three longnecks for the brothers. I take the opener with me, trying to escape being around the creep Preston any longer.

"Damn, now that's service." Merek slaps my ass.

"Stop." I swat away his hand.

"What's wrong?"

I don't want to cause trouble with my new job before it practically starts, but I also don't want Preston thinking I'm just fresh meat on the crew for the taking.

"See that guy at the bar?"

Marvel cranes his neck. "Yeah, that's Preston. He's on our crew. Worked with Challis and I today."

Merek clutches the back of my thigh. "What about him, Verde?"

"He's a dick, that's what. Saw you nuzzling up to me and thought he could treat me the same way."

My fear comes to life as Merek stands from his chair. I manage to push him down with the hand just holding a beer opener.

"I told him off, but you need to keep your hands off of me until my shift's over."

"He's fucking fired," Merek says.

"No, he's not." I slap him in the back of the head. "I'm a big girl and can handle my own stuff. I'm just saying less touching right now and as far as that goes during work on the ranch as well.

"I agree," Maverik pipes up.

"See, I'm always right. First thing you need to

know for this relationship to work out." I bend over and pop off the tab of each beer and then kiss his forehead before I walk off.

"What the hell?" he yells after me. "You just totally contradicted yourself."

"I'm always right." I shrug my shoulders.

Chapter 11

Merek

"I'll break his fucking legs if you don't let me fire him."

"Cool your jets, Merek. With Challis's looks he won't be the last guy to pick up on her," Maverik says.

"No shit, I need to buy her a gunny sack to wear."

"She does have nice tits." Marvel tips his beer back.

His words cause me to choke on my own beer. For years, I've worried the boy was going to be playing for the wrong team, but clearly he has a fascination for my girl's tits. *Did I just use the phrase 'my girl'?* And by damn if it didn't feel good.

"Touch her tits and I'll beat your ass, Marvel."

We all bust up in laughter at that comment, and I fucking shake my head at the conversation we are knee deep in and the feisty cowgirl I'm falling in love with.

"Talked to Saint on the way over here." My attention focuses in on Marvel. "He's agreed to pay us in three installments at the end of each month instead of at the end. How do we want to handle paying the hands since they think the money is coming at the end anyway?"

"We have to give them something to live on. It's not their fault our dad went and fucked up shit." Maverik slams down his beer.

"Guys." I set my hat on the table and run my hands through my hair and contemplate on how much to tell them about Challis's situation. "I've promised the money to Challis within forty days."

"You what?" They both say in unison, and even ol' Jake perks up from underneath the table.

"She's in a bind and needs it. We are going to hit local rodeos on the weekend. She's in a tough spot, guys."

And that's all I'm willing to share with them.

"Let's get real here, Merek." Maverik turns to me. "You've fallen a bit in love, have a hard-on for this girl, and expect us to fork over money to her when we are in a hardship as it is."

"Yeah, fuckface." Anger boils up in the back of my throat. "Like I'd ever ask that. I'm going to put my personal money in for you guys to pay. She can never know it's coming from me. Then in the end when Saint pays up, you'll just pay me back."

"Why don't you just give her the money?" Marvel asks.

"Because she's stubborn and prideful," Maverik answers for me. "I'm fine with that, but when she finds out the truth you're on your own, Merek."

"Deal," I say. "But she can never find out."

"What happens when she hears the other workers talking about money?" Marvel asks.

"I'll handle it. Plus, she's going to be pretty much on her own working the money colts that we need spot on."

"Mark my words, Merek, you are going to fuck this up."

"Thanks, Maverik."

I scan the bar searching for Challis and catch Preston staring at something pretty intent. And when I find out what he is staring at I instantly see red. Challis is bent over serving a table a large tray of drinks.

"Excuse me." I push back from the table and settle my hat on my head.

"Take it easy." I hear Maverik's voice and can guarantee he saw the same thing just go down.

I saddle up to the bar right next to the fucking puke.

"Merek Slatter, what an honor." He sticks out his hand to shake mine. "You're a great cowboy. I ride broncs as well."

I look down to his buckle and see he's wearing a high school state champ one and only smirk pitifully at it.

"So much as look at Challis again and I break both of your kneecaps. Try talking to her and I'll rip your head from your neck and shit down it. Any questions?"

I never take his hand but I wait for his response. None ever comes and I don't move from the seat, hoping to make the asshole uncomfortable as all hell.

"You can take her. I've got this under control," Tori hollers over to me. They were the only words I longed to hear and I don't waste a second.

In three long strides, I grab Challis by the waist, hoist her over my shoulder, and send the tray sliding onto the bar top.

"Thanks, Tori." I wave over my shoulder and slap Challis on the ass. Her squeals and laughter vibrate on my back as I carry her ass to the truck.

"Merek, stop. Put me down."

I snag the handle to the truck and toss her in the front seat.

"God, you're gorgeous."

She lets out a huff of air. "Yeah, real gorgeous with

my tits popping out and my shorts all tangled and this out of control hair."

"I'd take you right here and now."

She gives the *I dare you, boy* look and in seconds I pounce on her covering her body. And instead of pushing me away, she does the opposite and pulls me down into her. Her welcoming arms wrap around my neck and pull down to her until our lips meet.

"Merek."

"Yeah." I mumble down into her lips.

"I think I'm starting to really fall for you."

I smile against her lips. "I've already tumbled off the fucking cliff for you."

"I don't know if we're good for each other."

I run my hand down between us until I find her core, using my hand I gently rub up and down until I feel her squirm underneath me.

"I think we're perfect for each other and should live this out."

Challis throws her head back on my leather seat and lets out a moan as I undo her button and zipper. I slip my hand underneath her panties and rub once again. She fights to talk between moans of pleasure.

"Merek, we're going to wreck each other, and you're going to leave me for the road and one day I hope to go home."

I circle faster around her nub and then push two fingers inside her and feel her back arch up as she screams out.

"Let's do it. Be with me."

"I'm with you. Oh God, don't stop."

Her hips try to buck up under my weight as she rides out all of her pleasure, and within moments she melts underneath me and leaves me smiling as I stare

101

down at her flushed cheeks and bright eyes.

The sound of car doors shutting surrounds us.

"We have to get out of here." Challis tries to sit up in a panic. "It's closing time and we'll have an audience."

"I might like the idea of my hometown seeing me claim you, so they'll all back the fuck off."

"Merek." She pushes as hard as she can on my shoulders.

"Okay. Okay." I sit up, nailing my head on the roof of the cab. "Fuck, that hurt."

I try to adjust my raging hard-on in my jeans and watch as Challis studies each of my moves. If she weren't so horrified I'd give her the show of her life while she lay beneath me watching. Instead, I climb from the truck and make it to the driver's seat only to see Challis still sprawled out with her head in the driver's seat.

"Whatcha doing, Verde?"

"I'm kind of relaxed and never want to forget that."

I lean in and kiss the tip of her nose. "How about I remind you for the rest of your life."

"Promise?"

"Promise, Verde."

She lifts her head just enough for me to jump up into the driver's seat. I've never driven so fast back to Silver Star before in my entire life, even counting the times I outran the country sheriff and hid out behind Granddad's house.

I pull the ol' Dodge up the lane—lit and framed with white fencing—which I've done over a hundred times before, but this time something is different and I feel it in my gut. What I'm about to do is going to change my life forever, whether it be for the worse or for the better, but I have to roll the dice and bet on the better.

"Fuck," I growl out.

Challis pops up from my lap. "What?"

"The colts are out."

"Stop the truck." I slam it into park.

"I'll go get grain from the barn, round them up in the truck, and try to herd them my way."

She's out of the truck before I can object. I watch as my beauty bolts to the barn and is back in the lights of the driveway shaking a bucket of grain. I follow several colts walking up to her as she shakes the bucket of feed and can barely hear her talking to the horses. More and more of them group up as she walks toward the barn. I follow behind in the truck scanning the dimly lit areas for any strays. Once the herd is in front of the barn I jump out and shut the gate.

"There's thirteen out here and seventeen corralled out here." I can't see Challis over the herd of colts but can hear her clear as day.

"Let's start penning them. Don't worry about their stalls tonight. Just pen them up."

"Okay, I got to know them a bit. Bring them to me and I'll sort them off."

I listen for her directions and pick up on them quickly. It's clear this isn't her first rodeo as she sorts the colts into pens. I push them when she hollers and back off when I hear her code word. We work through them easily until only three are left and walk behind them, guiding the beauties to their pen and watch as Challis shuts the gate behind them and latches it.

She doesn't stop to make small talk, instead she walks up and down the pens, double checking the gates are latched and then goes for the barn to get feed. I watch dumbfounded as she starts feeding each pen and then reality finally sets in and I help her.

"This is fucking bullshit, Merek. Marvel and I triple checked each stall making a game plan for each colt, betting on which one would make the best horse on the track."

I grab her shoulders and pull her in tight. "Look at me, Challis, accidents happen."

"This isn't a fucking accident, Merek."

"Slow down, give me a bucket. I'll start at the other end and we'll meet in the middle."

I don't give her a chance to say yes or no before I set off to my end and begin to feed the horses. Thoughts of my dad sabotaging this whole plan fill my mind, but then quickly escape since this whole project is to save his damn ass. It had to be a mistake on Marvel and Challis's end, but by damn if I'll ever say that thought out loud.

As I near the middle set of square pens the rain begins pouring down on the brim of my hat. I look through the raindrops and I see Challis's figure nearing me. I look up to the clouds and laugh out loud at the downpour in Texas.

"Done. Got this pen, Verde." I wrap my arm around her shoulder and race back to the inside of the barn with her.

"It's okay. Shake it off. We have them all penned up."

"I hope your windows are rolled up." Challis stares out into the pouring rain.

I watch her under the eve of the barn and hurt for

her because I know exactly where her thoughts are. Her paycheck. Her ranch.

I snag her upper arm and drag her out into the downpour, and before she has a chance to protest I seal my lips to hers. I feel her hands grasping for me and they finally land on my shoulder and cheek.

"Merek, I can't lose this chance. It's my last one."

My lips seal to hers as I struggle to siphon all the worry from her.

"You won't. I'm here."

My lips go back to work on hers and get lost in the passion swirling around us. My hands find her ass and urge her to jump into my arms. She follows each of my commands. I back up until I find the fence and gently set her down. My shirt is ripped away from my chest and then I feel her nails dig into my skin. Either blood or rain dribbles down my chest as I continue to kiss the ever-loving fuck out of her.

A porch light flips on, distracting the both of us. I place my fingers over her lips. "It's a hired man." I nod in the direction of the porch, and then we both watch the arrogant asshole scratch his ass and then whip out his pecker and piss off the porch.

"Did he really just smell his fingers after scratching his ass?"

I bury Challis's head in my neck as she battles a fit of laughter. "Shhh. When he goes in, we are making a run for it."

I watch the asshole finish off pissing and then head back inside. I wait for the light to flip off before I feel comfortable.

Whirling around rapidly, I plant my back into Challis's chest.

"Jump on, Verde."

And in slow motion, I feel each of her limbs attach to me and it's as if the Gods above are trying to tell me to relish this moment.

"You on?"

"Yeah, Merek."

"Then nod your head and let the gate rip open."

"Oh, my God, you're so dumb."

"I'm not moving, Verde, until I feel that head nod."

The rain continues to pour down on us, drenching every single part of our bodies. I feel Challis nod her head and then a shower of giggles.

"Let 'er rip, Verde." I take off for my house, jumping side to side, and then lurching forward. Challis's squeals and laughter nearly make me lose focus, but it's a sound I want to hear forever so I keep her on her toes. Once we make it to my front steps, I'm out of breath, and Challis's laughter continues to fill the dark night.

"Let me down or I'm going to piss on your back."

"Can't say I've ever heard that before." I laugh as I lower her down letting her off my back.

"Oh, my God, Merek, I nearly pissed myself from laughing. What in the hell made you do that?"

She stands in the pouring rain, soaked clothes and drenched hair framing her face, and I nearly forget my name.

"Uh?" She pokes my chest.

"Just testing you to see if you fit in with the cool kids."

Her emerald green eyes light up, and I cover my nuts just in case.

"I just scored a ninety on that piece of shit bucking horse." She covers her mouth, containing her giggles. "I can't wait to see you run barrels."

"House now." I'm done fooling around and need her now.

Chapter 12

Challis

As Merek drags me into his living room, I replay locking the colts up and know I locked them up both times, and then vision myself piggy back on him and bust out into giggles.

"What's so funny?" Merek pulls me in closer as he drags his tongue up the length of my neck.

"Nothing." I lie and then let out another round of giggles.

This time he backs away in his dripping soaked state, throwing up both of his hands. "Give it up, Verde, what's so fucking funny?"

"Just wanting to know what the other judge gives me for riding that nasty bronc?"

"Nasty?" he questions.

I would've bet a thousand dollars I'd never see this silly, playful side of Merek. Not only does he give me a case of the giggles, but he also lightens all of my worries, and I finally feel like a twenty-one-year-old should.

"Yeah, I spurred the piss out of that rank bitch." I try to keep a sober face and then the giggles kick in.

"Seventy point ride."

His comment sobers me up and clearly my competitive side comes out to play.

"Really?" I plant both of my hands on my hips and may have accidentally unbuttoned my shirt in the process. "What does it take to get a winning ride?"

I feel myself being whirled around in Merek's living room and can't stop my case of the giggles. A stinging sensation lands on my ass as I'm guided into the kitchen, and in the next moment a shot glass is held up to my lips. The smooth whiskey pours down my throat. Another full shot glass is placed in front of me. I pick it up without thinking and raise it to the sweetest lips I've ever seen. Merek opens up and I tilt it back.

Another shot flows down my throat as my head swims in all sorts of emotions, and it hits me that Merek is before me because he genuinely cares about me.

"Another shot now," I say without thinking. I need something to drown out all the emotion before it eats at my core.

I feel the cold liquid flow down my throat as he tips up the shiny shot glass.

"Music," I demand. I need all the background noise from both of our lives drowned out.

We Are Tonight by Billy Currington begins to play throughout the house.

"Smooth move, Champ."

He raises both eyebrows back at me before chasing me around the kitchen. Merek's hands finally dig into my hips and drag me off to his room. It's a room I knew in the light of the day, but it's a new surrounding in the pitch dark.

"Merek," my voice comes out as a whimper.

"I'm here, Verde."

"I'm scared," I say in all honesty.

"Why?" His lips press against my neck as I stretch out, protecting myself.

"I...I've never done this."

I feel his body freeze just like I knew it would when the nasty secret left my tongue.

"Merek, talk to me." I die inside as each second

ticks by. "Merek."

This time it comes out as a scream and I feel my whole body being pushed back onto a mattress as his scent assaults my whole being. My fingers dig into his fucking jaw as the panic sets in. I'm ready to scream out his name again until I hear the tearing of paper and the snapping of a condom.

"Merek." This time it's more of a plea and a cry combined.

His fingers linger down my stomach and he slowly inserts a finger inside me. His finger dips and dives until I feel my own juices run down my inner thighs. It's like he was born to play me like a fiddle. Then Merek's tongue dips between my thighs lapping up my juices, and it's not until I feel him on me that I explode. I don't know if it's his fingers working me over or his tongue entertaining my sensitive skin.

"You say stop, Verde, but I want you right now."

Merek comes nose to nose with me, sinking his tongue in my mouth, and that's when I fully light on fire, needing more and wanting more from him. My hips instinctively buck up toward him but feel nothing. I repeat the action over and over, needing more of him. Merek Slatter dulls everything for me, and in this moment I need to get drunk on him.

I buck up one more time and feel nothing. Then I finally feel his sprawling palm on my hip pressing me down into the mattress. His touch is demanding and I obey. Holding still under him, I feel him fumble around for a second and then the pressure of him pushing inside me.

I'm not sure if I scream, cry, or moan as he inches his way in. I've always been tough, but this pain hurts and I can't take it anymore.

I clutch his face and force him to look down at me.

"Help me. This hurts." By the look of pleasure covering his face, Merek is feeling no pain at all. He pushes his hands up underneath my shoulder blades, cradles the back of my head, and then drops his forehead to mine.

"Look at me, Challis."

His movements still and I find the courage to open my clenched eyes.

"I can stop."

"No." I shake my head back and forth. "It hurts and feels good. Just go slow."

Merek's lips dip down until he's kissing the ever-loving hell out of me. His tongue dips into my mouth and mine meets his, and I get lost in the brewing passion between us.

Moments pass and I'm lost, drowning in an overload of sensations, and before I know it my nails are digging deep into his shoulders as he continues to work in and out of me slowly. I feel the same energy build up low in my belly.

"Don't stop," I pant out.

The pleasure is almost unbearable as I wrap my legs up and around his torso, wanting more and needing more, then I hear him grunt and look up to see his face. It's the look of sheer pleasure covering his face that I let go and spiral out of control.

"Merek."

I know I'm being loud but can't control it. He grunts as he pushes into me three more times and then collapses on me.

"Holy fuck," he whispers on the nape of my neck.

I chuckle and feel him push back in me and then lace my hands through the back of his hair.

"Was I okay?"

"No, better than okay. I don't think you'll ever have to worry about me straying."

I slap his back. "Well, that was romantic, asshole."

Merek rises up, taking me with him. "Well, it's the truth, and you told me to be honest."

"Real smart move on my part." I roll my eyes and let him drag me around the room.

"Best lay ever, and let me tell you, I've had my fair share of them."

"Enough. Enough. No more honesty when it comes to sex."

"So, was I really your first?"

He sets me down on the bathroom counter, the cold countertop causes me to shiver, and using my arms I cover my bare breasts.

I look down at my toes and mumble. "Yes."

"Fuck, you're making me hard again."

I use my foot to kick at his stomach. "You're such an ass."

"Hey, babe, got to live up to the rep."

I watch as he is so not ashamed of walking around the bathroom naked in front of me as he starts the shower.

"You know I'm halfway kidding. Just trying to relax your wound up ass."

"I'm not wound up."

"Really?" He mimics me by crossing his arms over his chest and then crossing his legs and looking down.

"Stop." I laugh so hard at the sight before me. "You look ridiculous."

"Well, so do you, Verde."

I leap from the counter and bound into the shower

before he has a chance to catch me.

"Ha, sucker, and I plan on using all the hot water."

"Oh no you don't." The shower curtain is ripped back and Merek steps in, and boy he wasn't lying about getting hard again. He pins me against the wall and attacks me—again.

Chapter 13

Merek

Traveling to rodeos may have not been my best idea to date. I've had Challis in my bed every night for the past two weeks and have had to watch her work her ass off on the ranch with the colts, so I thought this weekend rodeo would be a nice getaway for us. It was only a two hour drive from home but took us three and half hours.

I kept blaming it on Challis and her damn tank top and bouncing tits. I've always had an addictive personality, but something has unleashed inside me since falling for my wild cowgirl.

Sitting on the back of Maverik's tailgate, I try to zone in on the rodeo and the bucker I'm about to get on. Challis offered Mav to ride with us. Thank the good lord he did or my semi right now would be a full on raging hard-on. I can't keep my eyes off of Challis as she brushes Teebaby and braids his tail.

"Turtleneck," I yell over to her and she just flashes me a devilish grin. I'm only half joking but don't appreciate the fucking stares she gets from other cowboys.

Maverik steps in front of me. "Focus, dickweed, or that bronc is going to kick your ass."

I know he's right but by damn if I'll let him know that. "Let's roll."

I stand and grab my bag, but before heading to the back of the chutes, I walk over to Challis and wrap her up in my free arm.

"Merek, I think everyone knows I'm yours from your little show earlier."

"Just coming to get a kiss." I quickly peck her lips, knowing if I linger any longer I'll be in trouble.

"Can I watch you?"

I tilt my hat and give her a questioning look.

"I know some cowboys are very superstitious, so I'm just asking."

"Baby, talent has no superstition."

She rolls her eyes at my comment, and it may be the one thing I fucking adore about her. She's so modest and such a hard worker, where I have no problem showboating.

She gives me a quick peck, slaps my ass, and whirls me around toward the chutes. "Get out of here, Champ."

I grab my belt buckle and send her a wink. "Go get a seat, Verde."

Maverik grabs me by the shoulder and hauls my ass to the back of the chutes. One thing about my older brother—he is huge and tough as nails.

"Get your head in the game, bro."

"I've never felt better, Mav. I could spurt out a T-Rex right now."

"Simmer the fuck down." He slaps me in the back of the head and is the only man who could do that without getting his front teeth knocked out.

"You drew a good one. Let's make some money." Mav starts taping my hands up.

"Whatever I win tonight, I want it all given to Challis through a ranch check. I know she'd be pissed, but she's worked her ass off."

"No shit. Never thought I'd meet a harder worker than Marvel. She has two of those colts ready to run already."

"She can never know about this."

"You know what I think, Merek. Not good."

I ignore him like I usually do when he gives me good advice, and I begin stretching out my muscles and jumping around to loosen up. I do up my vest as the horses are loaded into the chutes. Something about the smell and sounds in the air once they're loaded fuels my addiction.

There's no greater high than climbing on the back of a wild animal and hanging on for eight seconds. The buckle and glory is just the icing on top. I make my way over to chute four and watch Mav get my rigging in place while I continue to pull my legs up in a spurring action readying myself. Unlike other times, I have a huge fucking smile plastered across my face as I scan the crowd for Challis, and when I spot her, the smile gets even larger. She's focused on my chute, and if I'm not mistaken, a bit nervous rocking back and forth. I've never seen my tough, little girl nervous. Not even working some rank colts or running full bore on Teebaby on the ranch.

I've been very clear about my feelings toward her, but she seems to always brush it aside or turn it into a joke. However, her rocking back and forth in the stands is probably the closest I'll ever get to her vocalizing her feelings.

The National Anthem is sung by a sweet little voice. I remove my hat and continue to rock back and forth staying ready for the ride.

I'm the last cowboy to ride, and with the score of seventy-two leading I feel pretty damn comfortable, but in this sport you have to draw the right horse to score high. I settle down on the black beauty, finding the right spot, throw my heels up on his shoulder, grab my hat, nod my head, and hang on for life.

I hear Maverik's voice in the background and then everything fades out as I spur and hang on. The horse is powerful, jolting every single part of my body. The smell of dirt flies up into my nostril as I stay centered and get the job done. I hear the whistle blow and go to loosen my riding hand, when I feel the horse stumble. My right side goes into the dirt first, and then it feels like a brick wall lands on me as I look up to see the horse roll over me. I fight to free my hand and scramble for safety.

My hand frees just in time before the mammoth rolls all the way over and is back up on his feet. As he scrambles to get up I feel a hoof on the inside of my thigh and the sound of my pants tearing. He pierces my thigh with one final push as he stands up and then sprays me with dirt as he takes off.

I prop myself up on my elbows trying to get up, but instantly get lightheaded. Maverik is out in the center of the arena at my side.

"Stand the fuck up and shake it off."

He loops an arm under one of mine as he pats me off. The crowd goes from deathly silent into an eruption of cheers. I tip my hat, and then spot Challis standing on her feet with her mouth covered. I raise my hat to her, waving it.

Once behind the chutes, another cowboy is on my side and they both limp me to the tailgate of the truck.

"You okay, man?" the one cowboy asks. "Need me to get the medics?"

"Nah, just got the air knocked out of me. Thanks, man." I stretch out my hand and give him a shake.

I feel liquid run down my leg, and when I look down it's not pretty. Torn jeans, a perfect imprint of a horse hoof, swelling, and a blood trail. The fucker broke skin. The shock of being under a horse is worse than the pain in my leg. It's something no cowboy wants to be faced with.

"Oh, my God, Merek." I look up to see Challis sprinting toward me.

"You need a damn turtleneck." I watch her perfect tits bounce up and down.

"Shut up. No joking. Are you okay?" She stops feet away from me.

"No, I'm dying." I raise an eyebrow. "I need your sweet lips on mine to restart my heart."

"Merek." She slaps me on the shoulder and I'm quick enough to catch her hand and pull her in for a long kiss.

"Jesus, I think you missed your calling, Merek." Mav steps with a handful of first aid shit. "You should work for Hallmark with all your fucking cheesy lines."

I tuck Challis in on my other side and let Mav go to work cleaning up the wound.

"Whatever, Nurse Nancy."

I lean over to kiss Challis again but get sucker punched right in the gut by Maverik.

"Oooomph."

Challis tilts my chin back to her. "You did kind of deserve that."

"Shut up and kiss me."

Her lips seal to mine but don't stay long. I think we both know it would be beyond awkward for me to spring an erection with Mav working on my inner thigh.

"What was my score? Fuck, I didn't even catch it."

"I don't know. I was too damn worried if you were

okay."

"Ninety-one. You won the round," Challis says.

"Told you I could ride a T-Rex, Mav."

Challis hops from my lap. "I'm dying again."

"Cowboy up, cupcake. It's my turn to show you how it's done, and I won't even get any dirt on my ass or tear my jeans."

Maverik laughs, and I can't help but chuckle too.

"Merek, I do believe you finally found your match in life."

"I think so."

I study Challis as she changes into her riding clothes and watch how she caresses and takes such good care of Teebaby. She's told me he is her best friend and if she ever had to choose between Teebaby and anything else that Teebaby would always win.

"She loves that horse."

Mav settles in on the tailgate next to me, handing me a longneck while tilting his back. "I've never seen a team like those two. Unstoppable. Quite a shame she didn't get a second chance to chase the national title."

"Fuck collegiate level, she's going straight to the pros after this shit storm is over."

Chapter 14

Challis

Teebaby jitters and is beyond antsy to chase some cans. He sees the arena and I have to hold him back until my name is announced. I pull back on him and he fights as he stamps his front feet in the dirt.

I line him up, check him to make sure he's only focused on the arena, and then let him go. He flies to the first barrel and takes it tight. My kneecap flies into the metal of the barrel, but it doesn't budge. We turn around that can and I look to the next, pushing him to go faster he takes can two as sharp and tight as the first one. He glides to the next one, a sharp pain in my lower back takes my breath away as he sits his ass down and turns. The pain is overwhelming and I try to stretch up easing the pain, but it doesn't work. My legs fly into action, hustling Teebaby home.

"Fifteen nine. Now that little cowgirl gave a whole new meaning to hustle."

I jump off Teebaby as soon we leave the arena and bend over trying to catch my breath, then stand up stretching out the cramp in my back. He tugs on the reins but I keep a tight grip on them, knowing he's hyped up from the run.

"Ma'am, you okay?"

An older cowboy steps up to me.

"Just a backache. I'm good."

It has to be from riding nearly ten hours a day at the ranch, or my daddy paying me back for always making fun of him when he'd hunch over with a pain in his lower back. That thought causes me to laugh. I can totally picture my old man sitting up in the clouds serving up payback for me, and I realize I didn't have a panic attack this time running barrels. I guess Merek Slatter may be my perfect distraction.

I climb back on Teebaby and stand up in the stirrups not brave enough to sit down and test the pain. Leaning slightly forward, I test my back trying to stretch it out.

"Challis." I turn to see Maverik out of breath. "What the fuck? Are you okay?"

I look at him dumbfounded.

"Talk before my brother drags his ass over here."

"Fine. It's just my back."

Maverik jumps up on the fence and sends thumbs up over to the bucking chute where Merek is perched. I offer him a weak smile.

"What the hell happened?"

"I don't know. About barrel two my back seized up with a cramp and it fucking hurt."

"Get down and stretch it out." He takes the reins from my hands.

I want to tell him that I've already done that but sitting in the saddle is killing me, so I jump down from Teebaby and stretch out again.

"Challis Jones, you're needed for the victory lap." Looking up, I see a rodeo director.

"Okay," I offer a feeble acknowledgment and climb back up on Teebaby.

"Take it slow," Maverik says. "I'll be right here when you get out."

"If you haven't noticed this horse has only one speed." I sit in the saddle and squirm for a bit. "Actually, I think it's gone."

"Back spasm from riding those colts."

121

The flag girl kicks her horse into action. A director standing by the gate hands me a bottle of whiskey. I grab it as I let Teebaby go. The bottle is raised over my head on the victory lap, and I don't even stop to look at chute one, instead I wait and look over at Merek, who's sitting on the last one and flash him a wink as I zoom by.

I don't miss his hoots of appreciation.

"Off the horse." Maverik stands at the gate. His voice is so serious I almost feel like I'm in trouble. I listen to his commands.

"Meet Merek back at my truck. I'll take care of Teebaby for you."

I walk alongside Teebaby with Maverik on the other side. "Um, no you won't. My back cramped. I'm not handicapped or a pussy."

"Fine, I'll help you."

I grab onto Teebaby's reins, ripping them from his hands and am instantly pissed off. "My dad didn't raise a woman who needs the help of men. I'm not helpless and can fucking do my own shit, Maverik. Thanks, but no fucking thanks. Nobody takes care of this horse but me."

He raises his hands in a surrendering motion and peels off toward the tailgate of his truck as Merek hobbles up to it.

"Verde." I hear Merek's voice.

"I'm fine. Let me do my thing."

I hear Maverik tell him to back off. Fucking lesson learned, never show pain in front of the Slatter boys. I'm not quite sure what enraged me with Maverik. I do know that I need to get better at accepting help in my life, but right now this is the only thing I have full control over and by damn if I'll ever give that up.

Traveling with Merek was a huge leap for me.

Some phantom pains shoot through my lower back, and I almost slip and grab it but think better of it. Instead, I snag four ibuprofens from the tack room in my trailer and go about cooling down Teebaby.

Once he's fed and I've put all the tack away, I walk over to Merek and Maverik with the bottle of whiskey in my hand.

I walk straight up to Maverik and hold out the whiskey. "Sorry, I just get a little wound up over rodeo and that horse."

"No offense taken, Challis, I get it, but just know you can always ask for help. Takes the strongest people to actually ask."

"Thanks." I drop my head and feel my arm being pulled into Merek.

"What was with all that cocky talk about not getting hurt or dirt on your ass?"

"I didn't get dirt on my ass."

"I know, you just magically got hurt sitting on a horse. Now that takes talent, Verde."

"Thanks." I grab his face and pull him close.

"For making fun of you?"

"Yes, I need you, Merek."

"Get a room, you two assholes." Maverik jumps from the tailgate. "I'm staying here tonight with you two. I'll sleep in the cab of the truck and let you two kids have the living quarters."

"Sounds good, brother."

We both stare as Maverik takes off.

"What in the hell?" I ask.

"Spotted a piece of ass," Merek responds as he nibbles on my ear. "Is that how it works?" I ask.

"Yep, and no woman can say no to a Slatter."

"I can."

"Really?" Merek challenges.

"Yep."

He stands and begins dragging my ass over to the trailer.

"How in the hell are you walking?"

"I'm tough."

I slap him in the back. "Seriously."

"Okay, I'm horny as fuck."

"Oh, my God, Merek Slatter, you're awful."

I can't help but laugh at his brash comments. He swings open the doors to the living quarters and hobbles in.

"Wait." I point to Mav's truck. "How is he driving us home in the morning when he has his truck here.

"Who knows with Maverik? He makes shit happen."

I climb up into the living quarters and fall on the couch. Merek is already sprawled out on the bed wiggling out of his jeans and is stripped down to his boxers. I'm beyond exhausted and feel no pain between the meds and shots I did with Merek and Maverik.

"Oh fuck." Merek sits up and grabs his thigh moaning in pain. I spring from the couch and I'm at his side in less than two seconds. He grabs me by the arm and pulls me down onto him.

"Told you that you can't resist a Slatter."

"You ass." I slap his chest and straddle him. I feel his hands roam up and down my thighs then travel up to the top of my jeans. I slowly begin to unbutton my shirt and seductively pull it off, with tank and bra to follow. I toss my hat onto the couch, making sure it lands the right way and then bend over placing my breasts in Merek's face. He's so distracted his hands go limp to his side as his mouth begins licking, sucking, and biting.

I could let him deliciously torture me in this fashion forever, so I force myself from Merek and stand up, placing my hands on my hips, full well knowing I'm going to jump back on that train in a matter of seconds.

"Now, what were you saying about not being able to say no to a Slatter?"

"Challis," he groans out, freeing himself from his boxers.

I unbutton the top of my jeans and pull them down just enough to expose my lace panties. "What were you saying, Merek?"

"You're right. Always right. You win. Now strip."

I giggle as I pull down my jeans and step out of them, and I take a bit longer dragging down my panties just to make him suffer. I crawl back on the bed fully nude and settle myself over Merek. He's always the one leading the way in the bedroom or stable, but not tonight.

"Did my little Verde find some courage?"

I don't answer him. As I slide down on him, the sensation nearly causes me to pass out. It's something I've never felt before. Merek's used to taking me and me enjoying it. I move my hips just the slightest and feel that ever-welcoming pleasure build up quickly. His hands firmly pinch each side of my hips as he starts guiding me up and down, forcing me to fuck him.

"Merek, slow down. I'm about to go."

He only grunts as he slams me down harder and harder. My hands find his hair and tug on it until he's

125

facing me in a sitting position. My lips attack his and my screams are muffled into his mouth as I spiral out of control.

Merek lifts me up and off him. I fall to the side and before I can ask what is going on I watch him grab himself and milk out his own release, and it hits me that he wasn't wearing a condom.

"Oh shit." It comes out breathy. "We got carried away."

"Just needed a little Slatter in you is all." Merek stands and begins cleaning himself.

"It's not funny."

The thought of me throwing everything away because of the emotions and passion I have for this man causes goose bumps to run up and down my arms. I know that I more than like Merek Slatter, but being knocked up could ruin everything at this point for me.

"Challis, I got you. I'm here for the long haul. I love you." He climbs into bed, collapses next to me, covers his eyes with his forearm and is out. I take it he had a couple more shots than I did.

The three words bounce off the walls of the small living quarters, and I have no idea how to react or feel, so I cuddle up to the only thing that's felt like home since my daddy dying.

Chapter 15

Merek

One Month Later

"Something is not right. First the colts were let loose, our feed order was misplaced, and now fences are torn down." I punch the side of the barn, knowing fixing the fences will set us back a good week.

"Smells like sabotage to me." Maverik saddles up his favorite childhood horse and gathers tools to fix the fence.

"We have to keep our heads in the game, guys," Marvel says.

"No shit. Do you not think we are aware of that?"

"I'm assigning some of the crew to security at night. This has Saint's name all over it. He's screwing with us so we don't get the job done." Maverik kicks his horse into a gallop and takes off to begin fixing the destroyed fence.

Between the fucking stress of saving the ranch, hiding my little cash flow secret from Challis, and her stressing over her daddy's ranch, I'm ready to blow up. We've worked the rodeo circuit every single weekend and kicked ass. The money flowing is a good thing only if I can get it to my stubborn ass woman.

"What in the hell happened?" Challis walks into the barn baffled.

I only shrug as I'm left speechless as well.

"We don't know, but it's not going to hold us back. We are working those five colts today since they're showing the most promise." Marvel begins to walk away.

"Hey, Marvel, I'm stealing Challis for a few hours."

He throws his arms up in the air out of frustration.

"No, Merek."

"I need a stress break. Please come ride with me."

"Marvel is about to stroke out. I can't."

"We'll be bringing in some cattle, so we'll be kind of working, and you can ride Teebaby for a while."

"Fine."

I know exactly how to play her heartstrings.

"I'm going to pack a quick lunch and then will meet you back here." I spin on my heels and head for the house, but before I hop up on the porch I holler back to her. "Saddle up Britches for me."

Challis just sends me the bird, which I know is an *okay, asshole.* I throw together a quick lunch and get hard just thinking about the alone time we'll have. It seems we have both been breaking our asses nonstop lately and some nights we are too tired to have sex.

I open the front door with our lunch bundled in a backpack and see the little shit walking down the trail in the direction of my favorite spot with my horse trailing behind.

"Challis."

She turns in her saddle. "What?"

"Forgetting something?" I raise my hands in the air.

I sprint and catch up with her, hopping up on Britches.

"To our spot?"

"You got it, Verde."

We both ride in silence and it's just the piece of mind I need right now. I haven't asked Challis how much money she has or how close she is to getting the ranch back. I've kept the cash flow going and her away from the rest of the workers. In fact, she's basically her own boss and probably could rival any of us Slatter boys on horseback.

We ride up the rolling hill where the pond sits and the scenery takes my breath away every single time. But today is different. I've told Challis I love her on at least ten different occasions, and she always manages to brush it off. It's never fazed me because I'll die trying for this woman. We've shared several wins together, injuries, laughs, and endured fights, but riding horseback with the woman I love to the place I adore the most in the world nearly turns me into a crying pussy.

We both hop off our horses in unison. I take the reins to Teebaby, which in all reality is a huge step for Challis, and tie our horses up to the willow tree.

"Here." I toss her the backpack.

"What do you want me to do with this?"

"Make me a picnic, woman."

"You're lucky I like you."

I fall down next to her in the tall pasture and pluck my sandwich from her before it's even finished being made and begin eating. I decide to go for the kill and see if I can crack Challis just the slightest. "Tell me about your ranch."

"I don't have one." She tosses all the stuff back in the bag and relaxes her head back on my side. Propped up on my elbow and relaxed on my good side, I slap her stomach.

"Talk."

"It's a ranch."

"Challis," my voice is full of anger.

"Fine. It's the Wine Cup Ranch in Fulton County. My dad quit riding bucking bulls when I came along, bought some land, turned it into a ranch, and started raising bucking bulls."

"And your mom?" I cringe, knowing something has to be behind this since she's never even broached the topic, but I'm finding out that I have to push Challis to open up.

"I don't have a mom. She left me at the hospital and called my dad to come pick me up."

I wince, not expecting that answer at all.

"I'm sor—"

"Don't be. She didn't deserve me or my daddy. He had to fight to get me from the hospital with all sorts of DNA tests and proof of having a stable living environment. Hence no more bull riding and the ranch."

She falls silent, still perched on me, and I immediately feel like a grade A dick for pushing her.

"Challis, I shouldn't have—"

"Stop." She swats my thigh. "If I didn't want to tell you, I wouldn't have. Want to know the meaning behind Wine Cup?"

"Yeah, I do." I run my hands through her silky brown locks. "Oh shit, your tattoo on your hip."

"Yep, that's our brand and got it after Daddy passed away. His signature is below it." She reaches up, finds my hand and interlaces her fingers with mine. "When Daddy bought the ranch there were only about four acres and a crappy old house on it, and the day he died it was over a thousand acres with his dream home on it. Anyway, he named it Wine Cup Ranch because he was always notorious for having a red solo cup in hand and said I was the finesse to the ranch, hence the word wine."

"He'd want you to have it, you know?"

"I know." Challis sits up, nudges me on my back, and then straddles me. "Thank you for being patient with me and being here distracting me. I haven't been able to give you all of me because I don't know what will happen when I lose the ranch."

I grab her chin, forcing her to look down at me. "You won't lose the damn ranch."

She shrugs her shoulders. "Sometimes I just wonder if I should let it all go and head down the road to rodeo with Teebaby."

"You could leave me and not think twice?" I whisper.

"I've learned not to get too attached to things."

"Let me up." I try hard to push her off of me without being aggressive. "Challis."

"Let me finish, Merek." She shoves me back down on the blanket. "But I fell in love with you, so my plan of traveling down the road doesn't really work either."

She stares down at me, and I'm sure I misheard her but don't dare move or ask question.

"Did you hear me, Champ? I love you."

"Say it again," I whisper.

"I love you, Merek Slatter. My body fell in love with you the night you walked into the bar. Your honesty has won me over, and your wild and free-spirited heart captured mine."

For the first time in my life, my smartass mouth is speechless.

"Is that a tear I see escaping your eye, Champ?"

"No, it's a fucking bug." I roll her over and cover the length of her body. "Thank you, Verde. You saved me from myself, and I'll love you forever for that."

"Saved a man-whore from himself, score." She tugs my face closer to hers and leans up placing a light kiss on my lips. "Love you."

I grind into her center as she widens for me, wrapping her legs around my waist. I try to sit up on my knees in the grip of her legs, unzip my pants, and drag them down. I reach behind me and unwind her legs and then begin removing her pants, dragging them down slowly and kissing her skin as it's slowly exposed.

My teeth graze her abdomen and then bite down on her panties, tugging them down. I give up halfway and pull them off in one fell swoop. Resting down on my elbows, I nudge into her entrance. "Oh fuck, I don't have a condom."

Challis's hips buck up into mine, and when I enter her it's fucking paradise that I never want to pull out of.

"You know a couple of weeks ago when I took the afternoon off?"

"Yeah, babe." I grunt as I work myself in and out of her.

"I got on birth control, and it's been long enough for us not to use a condom."

"Oh, fuck." I quicken my pace, not worrying how fast I blow. Challis's head arches back as she moans and tries to keep up with my rhythm. Watching her pleasure dance on her face and feel her tighten around me has quickly become my favorite addiction.

In one swift movement I roll over, so Challis sits atop me. I use my hands to guide her movements and before long she finds her rhythm. She plants her hands down on my chest as she continues rising up and down.

"I love you, Champ."

I grunt as I feel my release let go inside Challis.

Chapter 16

Challis

"Someone needs to call the fucking sheriff." I throw a rope across the barn. "This has gone too fucking far. We are weeks out from the big day on the track."

"What are you calling the cops on? Broken pipes?"

"Shut the fuck up, Preston." The man's face infuriates me. He's a dick to work with and I've kept my fucking distance.

He grabs my wrist and pulls me back. "Just because you're fucking one of them doesn't make you any higher on the totem pole, little girl."

I rip my hand away from him and see fucking red. "Don't you ever touch me again."

"What? You gonna sic your little boyfriend on me."

"No, I'll take care of it myself with my .223."

This is only the fourth time I've run into Preston, and if I was a betting woman I'd bet Merek did that on purpose.

"What's going on here?" Maverik steps up to us.

"Just trying to explain to miss all-star here that you can't call the sheriff about broken pipes."

"Fuck off and remember I know how to aim." I throw down the bucket of grain I'm holding and stomp off.

This is a total set-up. We've been set back around every single turn. Merek explained the debt of his dad's and who Saint really is. He sounds like a fucking charmer who rules the land with his dirty money. I know beyond a shadow of a doubt this is him fucking things up, and I'd bet he's deeper into shit more than money.

"You son of a bitch." Merek's voice startles me as I walk up to him. When I look up and see his fist cocked back and ready to nail his dad, I set off in a sprint.

"Merek," I yell before I get to him. "Stop."

My voice doesn't stall him at all and he takes a swing and misses. His dad lowers down and uses his shoulders, squaring up to take him out and he does. The two men tumble to the ground, rolling around with limbs flying everywhere.

"Merek."

The two men are so intense in the battle there's no way I can break them up. I turn back to the barn and start screaming for Maverik, who comes running out from the barn. He instantly spots the fight and dashes for the men. He yanks Merek up by the collar and the first thing I spot is blood flowing down his lip.

"You son of a bitch. Off this ranch now."

"What in the hell is going on?" Maverik shakes Merek by the collar.

"Tell him, oh sweet father."

His dad doesn't move a muscle as Merek continues to seethe and fight to get away from Maverik's grip.

"Tell him, you fucking coward."

"There's more debt." He steps back and wipes away his own blood trailing from his face. "This is only the first payment of five."

"And, you worthless asshole," Merek yells.

Maverik throws Merek behind and approaches his dad. He stands at least a good foot taller than him and makes his own dad cower down to him. I've never been afraid of Maverik until now. The angry steam billows off of him as he waits for his dad to answer.

"I put this ranch up as collateral, and now... Saint is coming for everything, even after he's paid up."

"Why on the God's green earth would he not be okay with just the money?"

"He caught me in bed with his old lady."

Maverik's fist sails into his dad's face with force I've never witnessed before.

"Pack your shit and leave now." Maverik steps up to his father who's bent over. "You're no longer welcome here. And tell Saint that fucker deals with me now."

Maverik turns to us. "Go get Marvel and tell him to stay with Mom and instruct him he's not to let her out of his sight. I'll take care of this piece of shit and you two deal with the broken water lines."

I grab Merek by the forearm. "It's your dad."

"What?" He peers down at me.

"It's your dad who has been sabotaging everything."

"Why would he do that when he needs that money?"

I shrug. "I don't know, but it's him. He needs this to fail for some reason."

"Well, he's gone, so nothing else can happen, baby."

I watch in horror as Maverik drags his own father off the ranch and boots him out on the road.

"Merek, something isn't right. None of this adds up."

"You're fucking telling me. I just want to be done with all of it. If we can get that first full payment then I can pay off the rest of the debt."

"But it's clear Saint wants blood."

"I'll fucking kill him before he gets to us."

I follow Merek to the barn and start moving colts around and am thankful Marvel and I have them grouped well. It's obvious the asshole who is stalling the operations has no idea who the good ones are, and for that it gives me hope and maybe it's a run of bad luck. I stop and watch Merek work. The man is beyond talented, the best bronc rider I've ever met, fixes anything, can ride and rope, and is hot as fuck to boot.

He catches me staring, and I can't help but smile back at him.

"Merek."

"Yeah, babe." He goes back to working on the exposed pipe.

"I have the money."

"Uh?"

"I've made enough money to go to the bank and get my daddy's ranch back."

This grabs his attention as he stands up from the place where he'd been working. "This weekend on our way to the rodeo we are stopping and getting your ranch back, Verde."

He takes two long steps and gathers me up in his arms. "Just remember, baby, as long as we have each other the rest of this shit is just noise."

"Merek, you've blocked out the noise for me, and now it's my turn to do that for you. I promise I'll be by your side until your mess is all cleaned up." I pause and think about how to word it. "I'm sorry about your dad."

"I love you, Verde, and so want to fuck you right here on this pipe."

"Always the romantic cowboy, aren't ya?"

137

Chapter 17

Merek

"Give me the fucking phone." I rip the phone from Challis's hand and wait for this Lola character to answer.

"Hey is this Lola? Yeah, well, Challis is on her way home to buy her ranch back. Meet her in town at the bank in fifteen. She's moving forward with or without you."

I pause, listening to the rotten bitch.

"Why, yes, I am her lawyer. See you in a few."

Challis is dead quiet the rest of the drive and I don't push her to talk. I crank up the radio and let our favorite playlist shuffle through as we drive back into her hometown. Her trailer is a bitch to pull into the parking lot and I tamp down the curse words I want to let fly as I park the truck and kill the engine.

I hop out and fix my hat and collar in the mirror. When I look back at Challis she's still frozen in the center of my bench seat.

"You ready?"

She turns to face me with a pale complexion and trembling figure. "What if this doesn't work out?"

"It will, Challis, and if it doesn't I'm paying the difference and you'll work it off for me."

"Merek, Preston told me he has only been receiving living stipends. Do you know anything about that?"

"Nope. All I know is you work fucking harder than any of those men and deserve to be paid more."

I tug her out of the truck, clutch her hand, and drag her into the bank. I talk for her as the banker prepares all the papers.

"Challis."

I turn to see where the voice is coming from, and when my vision spots Lola, I want to slap her. She's every man's dream with huge fake tits, a dark fake tan, and a fake smile. It's easy to see how her dad fell for her.

"Dear, looks like you've put on some weight."

I stand up and square off with the bitch. "You'll be talking to me from here on out. Don't you dare speak another word to her."

I feel Challis's body quake and then my blood really begins to boil.

"Well, you're Merek Slatter, aren't you?"

"Yes." My jaw locks, trying to keep in my true feelings.

"Well, you ran with my niece a few years ago. It was always off and on. Now hitting on ol' Challis."

"No, she's my girlfriend, and again, you'll keep your mouth shut." I grit out between my teeth as the banker returns with a stack of papers.

"Congrats, Challis, you've met all the requirements and Wine Cup is officially yours. I just need your signature in a couple of places."

Challis's hand shakes as she fights to finish signing her first name. I grab the pen, stopping her from finishing it. "You've told me over and over that your daddy raised a strong girl. Where is she now?"

Tears well up in her eyes and I just shake my head at her. I know it's what she'd want me to do...be the hard ass and force her to finish. She finally gives me a nod then goes back to signing, and this time it's with confidence.

She stands from the chair as the banker hands the

papers over to her. I take the keys from Lola and inform her she's officially off the ranch.

"I've been gone since the day he died."

Challis whips around and finally stares down Lola. I don't stop her and let her have her ending with the evil bitch.

"You never belonged there. You're a piece of trash and I feel for the next unfortunate victim who falls prey to your trap."

"I was good enough for your dad."

Challis goes into fighting mode, and I know this has been enough.

"Let's go." I wrap my arm around her waist and begin tugging her toward the door.

"Just remember Karma has your ass on speed dial, Lola."

I get Challis out into the parking lot. She twists around in my grip and starts swinging punches at me, landing a few on my chest.

"Whoa. Whoa." I hold my hands up and back away. "What the hell, Challis?"

"You slept with her niece. Out of all the fucking people in this world you fucking slept with Satan's bloodline."

"Challis, I have no idea who she was talking about."

"Hell, you've probably fucked her whole damn family." She slams her fist into the side of the truck. "I knew I should have never fallen in love with a man-whore like you."

"Are you serious right now?" I scratch my head, fucking lost with her train of thought right now. "Challis, I've been nothing but up front about my past. Sorry, I didn't keep a fucking diary of the names of the women. Are you going to look at me?"

"No, I'm done. I'm fucking done with all of this."

"Great. So, you get your fucking money out of me and the ranch and then just leave?"

She finally turns around to see me. "I can't handle any fucking more, Merek. I gave you my heart and fell in love with you and then to have Lola throw that in my face."

"Throw what? All she said was something about her niece. Jesus fucking Christ, I don't even know what to say right now." I walk around the truck and throw my bag over my shoulder. "I'll do you a favor and leave. Sorry I was such a piece of shit to you."

I walk away from Challis and expect to hear a plea from her, but nothing ever comes. If falling in love was the best feeling in the world, then this absolutely is the most rotten feeling I could ever have. Pulling my phone from my pocket, I call Maverik. "Where are you?"

"About to enter town. What did you forget this time, dumbfuck?"

"Nothing. I'm walking down the main drag. Pick me up."

"I'm still a good ten or so minutes out. What the hell happened?"

"Then I'll walk to the fairgrounds. Meet you there."

I end the call, not wanting to rehash what in the fuck ever happened. Now I wish I would've let Challis beat the ever-loving shit out of that woman. Pain and hurt races in my body and I ignore it.

I get to the arena before Maverik, throw my bag on the ground, sit on it, and realize this is what rock bottom feels like. I always thought rock bottom was going to be when I couldn't ride again or going broke, but I was completely wrong about all of that. It's when your heart is shattered.

The ringing of my phone pulls me from my nasty thoughts and when I look at the screen, it's Challis. It takes me several seconds to decide whether or not to take the call.

"Hello."

"Merek." My name rolls off her lips in a sob.

I don't know what to say to her, so I just listen.

"I'm..." I can tell she's trying to catch her breath on the other end of the phone. "I'm sorry."

The two words are a bit of a welcome to me, but I'm still beyond pissed about how easily she could have just written me off and was ready to walk away from me and from us.

"Say something, Merek."

Bending forward I bury my head in my free hand. "I don't know what to say, Challis. If you were so damn ready to walk away from me that easily, why would I want to come back?"

"I freaked out."

"No shit. You freaked out. Lola was more than likely lying and just played you like a fucking fiddle. I've never claimed to have a clean past, but I am sure of one thing, Challis Jones. I'm the best thing that's ever walked into your life and you just chose to throw it all away on a drop of a dime."

There's a long pause, and I'm proud of myself for not caving right back into her. She's my one true addiction, the reason I get up in the morning, and the person I wouldn't be able to live without, but I refuse to be a doormat to anyone.

"You're right. I freaked out. I told you I suck at relationships, and all this built-up stress has done me in. I'm sorry."

"I suck at this relationship shit too, Challis, but I'd never throw you away fucking ever. I love you, and when you love someone you don't treat them like you just did me."

"I love you too, Merek," she whispers.

And it seems we are at a crossroad. I'm still furious with her and don't even want to see her face right now even though I love her and want her forever, but what she did hurt me.

"Bye, Challis." My thumb pushes the red circle ending the call. As soon as I do, I hear the distinct sound of Maverik's truck pulling. He parks right next to me and looks down at me out the driver side window.

"Rough day, partner?"

"You have no fucking idea."

"She find out about the money?"

"Oh, hell no. Her fucking stepmom or whatever the hell she is made some comment at the bank about me running around with her niece a while back, and Challis blew off the fucking handle claiming to end everything."

"C'mon, little bro." Maverik steps from the truck and goes to the back of it. I hear the squeak of the metal as he slams down the tailgate.

I follow him and plant my ass down. Maverik takes a seat next to me and hands me a beer. He must know it's pretty bad because he's always the one harping my ass about drinking before riding.

"Do you love her?"

"I'm not going to answer that."

"Why?"

"Because fucking of course I love her." I take a long

pull from the beer bottle.

"Put yourself in her shoes. No family at all, working her ass off to save the ranch she grew up on, her body is sore as hell from training colts. She falls in love with the bad boy of rodeo, and then the one person she despises in this whole world digs at her one final time with the fact you fucked her niece." Maverik cracks open his second beer and isn't shy about putting it away.

"That gives her the excuse to blow up at me?"

"Think about it, dumbshit. Just for a minute, step back and think about it. Who else does she have in her life? Who is she going to go running to? Yeah, she has her aunt, but you know damn well how stubborn and bullheaded she is. You were an easy target."

Maverik's words sink in and I crack open a second beer, downing it within seconds. He's right.

"She called me to say sorry."

"And what did you say?"

I just shrug and think about how I ended the call without saying a goddamn thing to her. I pull my phone from my pocket and redial her number, but she doesn't answer. I try her number three more times and no answer.

"She's not answering."

Maverik takes his hat off and scratches his head. "Just for once, I wish you fucking kids wouldn't be so damn bullheaded and just work things out. Guarantee you she went home. To a ranch that she now owns but has nobody because you are too fucking stubborn to work shit out."

"Let's go." I slide from the tailgate. "She pointed out the ranch to me on the way here."

Maverik holds up his beer. "I'm not driving and

you most certainly aren't either. You know the cops will be all over our asses."

"I'll find someone. Let's go."

I scour the back of the chutes and finally find a teenage boy who can drive us.

"Merek, you don't have enough time."

"I'm making time, Maverik. Are you in or out?"

He slides into his back seat with a fresh beer, pissing and moaning about the whole situation.

"Are you a local?" I ask the young man.

"Yes, sir."

"Don't fucking call me sir and take me to the Wine Cup Ranch."

"Um, sir…" He stops himself. "I mean, Merek, that ranch has been deserted for months now."

"Just fucking drive." I lay two one-hundred dollar bills on the seat between him and me.

The drive is hell and seems like it takes an eternity. Wine Cup is on the other side of town and at least ten miles out. As we get closer and closer, awful, nasty thoughts begin to fill my mind.

"Stop." Maverik knocks me in the back of the head.

That damn man can read me all too well. When we turn down the driveway the first thing I spot is the large archway with their brand on it and then far off in the distance I see her lime green truck.

"There. Take me there." I point to the truck. "And haul ass."

The young man follows my directions to a T, causing gravel to fly as he gets after the gas pedal. I'm out of the truck before it comes to a stop. Teebaby is still in the trailer and I begin shouting her name and get no response.

The corrals are empty, haystacks tipped over, and

tumbleweeds occupy every nook and cranny of the place. It's the picture-perfect ghost town. Just a skeleton of a once has been ranch. I check barns, stables, and even open the door to the house and holler in.

The inside of the house is the most heartbreaking. I take a step in and pick up the picture that's propped up on the foyer table. It's a five-year-old toothless Challis smiling back at me from the top of a pony, with her dad smiling right back. She's holding a trophy. My eyes scan around the house, and picture after picture is of Challis, and in each one she's on a horse with her dad right along her side.

One photograph sticks out to me and it's of Teebaby and Challis. A birthday scene lay in the background with a large cake, balloons, and friends, and then there's her dad leading Teebaby off a trailer and Challis standing frozen covering her mouth. A set of chills run up and down the length of my spine as I study the cases of buckles, mostly of her dad's from bull riding. But I'm haunted by the fact that every single picture she's standing right next to her dad from birthdays to graduations.

"Merek."

The sound startles me as I whirl around with the picture of Challis and Teebaby in my hand. It's Challis with red, puffy eyes that are nearly swollen shut.

"I have nothing." Tears flow down her rosy cheeks. "I have the ranch back and lost you. Look around. I have nothing."

She falls to her knees in the entryway and begins wailing.

"Hey, hey, hey." I fall down right next to her, dragging her into my lap. "I'm here. You have me,

Wine Cup, Teebaby, my brothers, and Silver Star. It will all be okay."

"I worked so hard my whole life to end up here and have fucking nothing."

"Challis." I pull her head up and force her to look at me. "You have me, and together we can have everything."

"You left me."

"Baby, you pushed me away. You were angry and said things, but look where I am. I'm right here. I'm not letting you go, Verde."

She breaks into another fit of sobs, and each time her body racks against mine and I have to fight to hold it together. I never thought I'd see the day where my feisty little cowgirl would break down.

"The bitch moved my dad's body."

"What?"

"His grave is all dug up and the headstone is gone."

I hold back all of my emotions, trying not to add any fuel to fire, but I will be having words with Lola.

"I'm here, that's all that matters. We'll get everything back, and for fuck's sake we'll run bucking bulls if you want." I readjust her in my lap so she's straddling me and looking straight into my eyes. "We have a clean slate and can build whatever empire we want. Our future is endless."

Challis melts into my body, tucking her head into my neck. "I'm so sorry, Merek. I was lashing out, and really, I don't care if you boned the Tooth Fairy. Just never leave me again no matter how big of an asshole I'm being."

I laugh hard and finally relax just a bit. "I've fucked the countryside but never ran into the Tooth Fairy."

We sit in silence for a long time, and I let Challis

cry and just hold her. As much as I want to tell her to knock it off because it's killing me, I don't. I know she needs this release and probably to learn to show these emotions more often instead of blowing up.

Footsteps enter the house. "You two going to rodeo or sit around and cry like pussies all day?"

Leave it to Maverik to keep shit real like he always does.

Challis lifts her head from my shoulder and shrugs, silently asking me what I think.

"We need to go to the rodeo and do our thing. Hell, your hometown needs to know you're still alive and ready to kick ass."

"What if Lola's there?"

"You won't look or talk to her. Her ass is mine."

Challis tries to stand but tumbles right back on top of me. Clearly her legs aren't ready to steady themselves. Maverik holds his hand out to her and she takes it.

"My brother can be a dick, Challis, but just so you know you now have two other brothers in your life who'd love to kick his ass any day for you."

"Thanks, Maverik."

Challis throws him off guard by wrapping her arms around his neck, pulling him into a hug. My body is stiff and I do my best job of sliding back up the wall off the cold tile ground.

"I'm taking this one." I pull the toothless picture of Challis off the wall.

"Let me see that." I pass it to Maverik and he erupts into laughter.

Challis snags the picture and holds it to her chest. "Hey, we all go through a bit of an awkward stage.

"Thank God you grew out of it." I slap her ass and

guide her down the front steps.

"Um, who is that?"

"Some kid Merek paid to drive us here."

Challis looks confused. "Don't worry about it."

Challis and I hop in her truck and head back to the fairgrounds. I told Maverik to stop at a fast food place and grab us some grub. I study Challis as she drives us back into town with her game face plastered on and strong spirit well and alive. The sun shines off her dark brown hair and lights up her fire green eyes, and it's in this moment that I know beyond a shadow of any doubt that I'll be making her Challis Slatter before it's all said and done.

Chapter 18

Challis

Part of me wishes Merek would've said we were going back home to Silver Star instead of insisting on going through with the rodeo. My eyes still as my heart aches and my pride feels beyond foolish. I can count on one hand how many times my own dad saw me cry. Crying and having meltdowns isn't in my vocabulary or the way I roll.

The haunting sight of my dad's grave dug up with fresh dirt strewn everywhere is a sight I'll never forget, and I can only hope that if I see Satan tonight I'll be able to hold my emotions.

"You okay?" Merek asks as I pull into the fairgrounds.

I pull down my aviators and give him a shrug. It's a bittersweet feeling pulling into this place. It was my playground growing up. We spent more time here at rodeos than we did at home.

There's a long line of trailers waiting to get into the parking behind the chutes.

"Merek, you better get out and get to the chutes."

"Nope, not until you're parked."

"Don't be stubborn."

We inch up in line and that's when I see it. A brand new archway sprawling across the entrance with the words "Cody Jones Arena" in the center. I fucking lose it again with all sorts of different streams of tears flowing everywhere.

"What an honor, Verde. Your dad would be damn fucking proud of you coming back here and running."

He grabs my hands and clutches them in his.

"You can't leave me, Merek. You're the only thing I have left."

"I know. You're screwed."

I bust out in laughter and shake my head at his cocky ass. I pull up to a parking attendant in crazed laughter with tears rolling down my cheeks as if I was the poster child for "Hot Mess Train Wrecks".

"Go ahead and park where you'd like. Make sure to leave openings."

"Got it. Thanks."

"Pull up next to Maverik's truck."

"But I always park a row behind you guys."

"You're mine now and I'm the boss, so listen."

"Whoa there, pony, I don't remember mentioning anything about you being the boss."

I listen this time and pull up right next to Maverik, who has food spread out on his tailgate along with Merek's riding gear.

"Let's go. You drew a good one."

Merek hops out and follows Maverik. He stops and hollers over his shoulder. "Watch me tonight."

"Hell no."

"Please."

"No, Champ. I'll be right here eating. Hurry up and go."

The announcer is just welcoming the fans and I know Merek is pretty screwed, but also know there's no way I could talk him out of riding. I haven't watched him since the first time when the horse rolled up on him. Call it bad luck or a weird superstition, but it was almost like I caused it to happen.

Now, I have my own ritual while he rides. I put on our favorite playlist and listen to our favorite country songs, trying to drown out the background noise. I wait for his name to be announced and then pace back and forth by my trailer until his score is announced and so far so good.

Good Girl by Carrie Underwood comes on and I sing along as I busy myself until I hear his name. Three or four riders go by before I hear his name and the crowd goes absolutely wild, and every single time it makes me smile to know that the World Champion is all mine.

"In chute one, Merek Slatter will be spurring one out as soon as he settles in."

Laughter erupts from me and I shake my head, "Funny one, Dad."

It's a sign to fight like hell to make it work with Merek. The sound of the gate crashing open is the next sound I hear and the pacing begins. I sing the words to the song, focusing in on the beat. The roar from the crowd is so loud I can barely hear my own words.

Then everything goes deathly silent and I freeze. Moments feel like years, but I can't move. "Medics to the arena."

"No. No. No." I race to the back of the chutes, taking the shortcut I did as a young child, jumping from pen to pen until I'm standing at the back of chute one. The scene is insane with the ambulance already pulling in the arena and a swarm of cowboys huddled in a circle. I notice one of the pickup horses is short a rider.

Without thinking, I leap down into the chute and take off for the center of the arena.

"Ma'am, you can't be out here."

I turn to see my dad's best friend, Frank, and just

keep running.

"Merek."

I near the circle and keep screaming his name. Maverik pulls me back away from the scene.

"Let me go."

I kick and scream with all might.

"Merek."

I see a figure stand straight up and it's Merek. He's one of the men huddled around the circle, and when we make eye contact I'm relieved and confused.

"It's a pickup guy. Crashed into a bucking horse and is beat up pretty badly." Maverik continues pulling me out of the arena.

"Merek."

"He's fine, Challis, get your ass out of the arena before you get fined for not being in proper dress code."

I relax with his words and pull away from him and begin following him out the arena.

"Holy shit." I breathe out.

"Merek is fine and will be fine. I suggest you go to your fucking trailer and get your head on straight."

I exit the arena and kick dirt up as I walk back to my trailer. The sight of Teebaby is everything I need to see. The familiar surroundings, the arena being dedicated to my dad, and Merek standing and walking all sink in at once. Leaning on Teebaby, I run my hands through his mane and know everything will be all right. Not always pretty or typical, but all right. And I'm good with that.

I go about getting ready to run barrels and don't miss the stares of familiar faces staring me down but not stopping to talk. Childhood friends pass as well as rivals from my high school days, and I'm thankful some of them only offer weak waves and move on. I have nothing to say to them and don't want to hear any "I'm sorry for your loss."

When I moved in with Aunt Tori it was heaven in that aspect because no one knew me or anything about my past. Dust flies from Teebaby's saddle blanket as I toss it up on his back. His saddle flies easily on his back, and I go about cinching him up and putting on his ankle braces.

"Hey, sexy."

I look behind me and see Merek nursing a longneck on the tailgate of the truck.

"Not funny." I point straight at him. "Don't ever scare me like that again."

"It'll take more than a rodeo accident to drag me from you."

I shake my head and turn back to Teebaby, giving him some fresh water.

I walk over to Merek and take a drink of the ice cold beer. "Want to help me change?"

"Fuck yes, I do."

He drags me to the living quarters and strips my tank top off and fumbles with the button of my jeans. I attack his lips, kissing him hard and trying to pour everything I have into him. I'm bare naked before him. My fingers fumble with the button of his jeans, and clearly I'm not fast enough for him as Merek picks me up and tosses me on the bed.

I watch as he unbuckles his buckle and then his pants. His zipper goes down slowly. I raise up just enough to grab his shirt and rip him down onto me. With my other hand, I reach down and grip him, guiding him into me. And that's all it takes for my bad boy to start working in and out of me. I clutch at his face, digging into his flesh as he relentlessly takes control of me.

He rolls over, leaving me to sit on top of him.

"This is my favorite view in the whole world."

I slap his chest and begin to slowly move back and forth on top of him. It's always the sweetest sensation and brings me to the edge quickly. His fingers dig into my hips as he begins to control my movements. The veins in his forearms pop out as he growls. Gripping onto his shirt covering his chest I let go and spin out of control, screaming his name.

Merek covers my mouth and lets out a chuckle. He flips me over again, rolling me to my stomach and then covers my body. My ass automatically backs up pushing into him, and then I feel him cover my back and then feel his breath in my ear.

"You mean more to me than rodeo, gold buckles, and glory, Verde, marry me."

He pushes his World Champion buckle in front of my face as he growls out his pleasure one last time. I feel him fill me as he slowly pumps in and out of me. Tears fall from my eyes and land on the buckle.

I feel his lips nibble at my ear and his hand runs through my hair.

"I'll marry you, Champ," I whisper. "I love you."

Merek rises from me and starts to clean me up and dress me as I lay in the bed with his buckle clutched to my bare chest. When it comes to my bra, he grabs the buckle and I hold it tighter to me.

He chuckles at me. "Move your hands, you need to get dressed."

"You're not taking this back. It's mine."

His lips meet mine. Merek gives me the sweetest kiss, and it's one to remember, as most of ours are either passionate or quick pecks. He rolls off me, holding out his hand, and then pulls me up.

"Now get dressed. You gottta show your hometown that you're part of the cool kids club."

"Funny, ass."

I unclip his buckle from his belt and toss the belt in his direction.

"Good luck winning another one."

"I have an extra in Maverik's jockey box. Love you, Verde."

Merek ducks and jumps out of the trailer. I'm left sitting half dressed on my bed running small circles over his gold buckle. Not just any gold buckle, but the World Champion one that he wears every single time he rides or goes out anywhere. He gave it to me. I know if the man could take his beating heart out of his chest and give it to me he would. This is as close as he can get.

I hustle up and get dressed, tossing my old buckle on the bed and strapping on my new one. It makes me feel like a new person and it's almost like we both took our vows lying their making love. I'll never need anything else from Merek as far as a promise or a ring.

When I step outside, I don't waste any time finding Merek or dicking around. Instead I jump up on Teebaby and head toward the arena.

"How does it feel to be back home?" I reach down and pet his mane. "There's a new man in my life, but you'll always be number one."

I reach the entry gate as the barrel racers begin to line up. I've drawn the last hole and take the time to warm up my amped horse. He could really do this with his eyes shut with cold muscles. His blood bleeds barrel racing and it's the one thing that's been my savior.

"Let's give a friendly welcome to a hometown cowgirl. Anyone remember a certain brown-haired feisty one that goes by the name Challis Jones?" I'm in shock when the crowd goes wild. "I've seen this girl grow up in the rodeo scene and would hate to tell you cowboys that she could out ride any of you. Her daddy was the great Cody Jones, and he raised one hell of a kid.

I fight back the tears at the mention of my dad's name and the atmosphere of my favorite arena. I take a split second to look over to chute one and see Merek sitting on it. "Nice, Dad, I guess you approve," I say to the air.

Pulling back on the reins, checking Teebaby, I give him a few seconds to get hyped up for his run and then I let him go. I let it all go, the heartbreak and fears. He floats us around barrel one, sits his ass down on barrel two taking it tight, whirling around barrel three, he takes it too sharp tipping the barrel forward. I reach out with my hand as I whirl by it and shove it in the opposite direction. The last sight of the barrel I see it rocking back and forth. I urge Teebaby home, not even looking at the time on the scoreboard. I know for a fact that was our fastest run to date.

"And ladies and gentlemen, there's our first place cowgirl running a fifteen flat."

The flag girl nods for me and I follow her in for the victory lap.

"Hey, can you go the opposite way? I have someone I want to pick up."

"Sure." Question covers the teen's face.

We race up to the chutes and I stop for a second in front of Merek and Maverik.

"Get on, Champ, I'll take you for a spin."

Merek doesn't question me as he hops on the back and holds on. I nudge Teebaby into a run and then let him go, taking an extra lap and enjoying the moment my daddy set up for me. He may have left me, but he made damn sure I found my place in life and the perfect man to live out my story with.

"Well, that was quite romantic." Merek kisses my neck.

"Just showing you how it feels to fit in with the cool kids, Champ."

I feel his hand cover my buckle and then his teeth bite down on my neck.

I dump him off at Maverik's truck and go about cooling and settling Teebaby in with a permanent grin. That was the fastest run I've ever made in that arena and can't help but think my daddy had something to do with it. A sense of peace washed over me as I ran those barrels and saw Merek watching me from chute one.

"Verde."

"What?" I can't see Merek since the trailer is between us.

"Want to go out tonight or you too tired?"

"Yeah, sounds perfect."

I hustle up a bit picking up all my tack and then change my shirt into a tight fitting black V-neck knowing it will drive Merek wild. I tuck the front of it behind my gold buckle. Looking in the mirror, I can't help but stare at it and how perfectly the black shirt frames it.

"Move your ass, Challis," Maverik growls from the

outside of the trailer.

"I'm coming, just a second." I grab a hair tie and sweep all my hair off the side and begin braiding it as I throw open the door to the living quarters. Merek and Maverik are so not patiently waiting.

"Just let me finish this braid."

"Hurry up, I need to get my drink on," Maverik responds.

"Well, someone is sure antsy. What the hell is up with you?"

He just shrugs as I tie off the braid and hop on Merek's back.

"Giddy up, baby."

"Where we going, Maverik?" Merek asks.

"There's a bar and street dance across the road."

I bite down on the tender flesh of Merek's neck and then kiss around it.

"I don't think you want me popping a boner right now, Verde."

I laugh hard when I see Maverik shake his head. Before we cross the road I hop down from Merek's back. The crowd is huge and I spot several familiar faces. The main road is shut down with a band playing in the intersection. The aroma of beer and whiskey fills the air and I instantly become thirsty.

"I need a beer, Champ."

He grabs my hand and starts weaving through the crowd. Several friends from high school send me a quick wave, but then flat out ogle Merek. He notices me bristle up and just shakes his head.

"Let's just have a good time tonight," he hollers in my ear.

I nod and wait to the side while he and Maverik order drinks and take a double look when I see a gorgeous blonde whose hand is tucked in the back pocket of Maverik. I've seen girls swarm and flock the man but never actually touch him. He typically takes off and has his way with women behind closed doors.

"Here." Merek hands me two beers.

I stand up on tiptoes and yell in his ear over the racket of the band and crowd. "Who is that?"

Merek looks at me weird.

"Who is the blonde on Maverik?"

"Oh, that's Ella, his old high school crush."

"She doesn't seem super friendly."

"She and I don't see eye to eye. She crushed Maverik years ago and I told her off the other day when I ran into her."

"Where?"

"In town. Guess the bitch is home for a bit."

"Merek," I scold.

I try to process all of it but feel Merek press my cup to my lips and smile.

"Bottoms up, Verde."

I pound the first beer and the ice cold golden liquid is refreshing and tasty. I nurse the second as a small crowd swarms up, mostly interested in Merek. I keep stepping to the side or behind him, but he finally pulls me to the front of him, pressing my back into his chest and keeps me there.

The sad thing is I know several of the people around us but have no desire to talk to them. I was never the social butterfly because I was always working with my dad or riding Teebaby. All my rodeo friends are off at college tearing it up, not here at home.

My buzz quickly takes over and I get lost in the old time country music. I sway back and forth in Merek's arms as he entertains the crowd. Maverik hands me two shots of whiskey, leans over, and yells in my ear. "To my new sister."

He raises both our shots and we slam them together one at a time. My face curls up as the whiskey burns going down.

"Chase it with your beer," Merek's voice is in my ear.

"I want to dance."

A Patty Loveless song comes on and I'm dragged out to the dance floor before I know what's going on. Merek takes the lead and I just follow two-stepping right behind him. Song after song we dance the night away. Merek even gets a little funky grooving to some modern upbeat songs. The man has moves. My dad's best friend, Frank, grabs me for one dance and whirls me around.

"Your dad would be damn proud of you."

"Thanks, Frank."

"I need my little lady back."

Merek hauls me over to a picnic table and sits me down.

"You need to eat and soak up some of that alcohol."

"I'm not even drunk." I raise my hands, knocking over two glasses of water.

"Not even, baby."

***

"I'm never drinking again." I roll over and slap Merek's bare stomach.

"You know you say that every single time."

"How do you not even feel sick? You out drank everyone last night."

"I'm a stud."

"My stud." I pat his abs again. I roll up on my elbow and stare down at my guy and then realize I'm naked.

"Um, where are my clothes?"

Merek opens one eye. "Somewhere at the street dance. You started stripping."

"Shut up, you liar." I pause for a second. "Really?"

"No." He laughs and pulls me on top of him. "You insisted on having sex with me and instantly stripped when we got back."

"We had sex last night?"

"Four times, Verde."

"I was kind of drunk."

"Yes, you were."

"I needed last night. It was fun."

"Yeah, we need to cut loose more often, Verde."

I place a sweet kiss on him and then bounce up and stumble like a naked fool around the living quarters.

"What's the hurry, Verde?"

"You know what happens when our naked bodies mingle too long, and I need some greasy, spicy food to kick this hangover's ass."

"Just take another shot. It's the best cure."

"Fuck you." I slide on my jeans, fasten my buckle, and slide on the same black shirt. Aviators and a messy bun are next and I step out in the bright sun and moan in pain.

"Not so tough this morning?" Maverik asks.

"Holy loving hell, I might die."

I look around to see everything picked up and Teebaby already loaded.

"I figured you wouldn't be up to too much work

this morning."

"Thanks, Mav."

"Not a big deal. I couldn't sleep anyway." He plops down on his tailgate.

"Everything okay?"

"Sure is, little sister."

"Who was that gal with you last night?"

"Just a friend."

I know something is up, but I'm sure as hell not going to push the man.

"Well, thanks. Now go get your brother going. I'm damn hungry."

I moan and rustle in my sleep as Merek drives us back to Silver Star. The greasy food did the trick, but now my stomach is rolling.

"We are almost home, Verde."

"I feel like shit."

"Still hung over?"

"No, I feel pukey though."

"Five minutes."

I lay my head back down on his thigh and enjoy the feeling of his palm rubbing up and down my abdomen.

"What in the hell?" Maverik accelerates the truck, causing me to nearly roll off the bench and into the stick shift. "Oh fuck, it better not be."

I pop up from the bench and see a black sky of smoke and it's centered right over the ranch. Merek takes the turn up the driveway way too fast and I almost scold him because of Teebaby in the back.

Sure enough, when we pull up one of the training barns is up in complete flames. I catch sight of Marvel, who's doing his best of running colts out, and before I know it, I'm out of the truck and running into the barn unlatching pens and shooing the colts out into the open. They take off as soon as they hit the open air.

I go back in for the third time but am pulled back by a fireman. Looking behind me, I see Granddad and Merek's mom standing on his front porch.

"This is fucking it. I've had enough of this bullshit."

"Merek, no."

"Me too," Marvel pipes up.

Maverik pulls a shotgun from the back of his truck. "Let's go take care of business, boys. Nobody fucks with the ranch like this."

He hops in his truck and the other two brothers follow him. I scream Merek's name over and over, but he doesn't look back nor gives me a second thought.

"Son of a bitch." I throw a rock at the back of the truck as they peel out of the driveway.

"Let them go, Sis." I turn to see Granddad standing by my side. "You're not going to stop those boys. This is war now." He loops his arm in mine and walks me up to his porch. "I see you won a new buckle."

"It's Merek's."

"Oh, sweetie, I know. I take it he asked you to marry him."

I look over at him baffled and wonder if he's a mind reader or if the guy knows everything.

"Since he won his first buckle at his first pee-wee rodeo he always told me he was never giving his future chick, his words not mine, a ring but his favorite buckle."

I laugh at the story and feel a little more at ease

Chapter 19

Merek

"Get your ass out here, Saint."

Maverik fires off a shot into the air. We had to bust through two gates, leaving Maverik's truck billowing with steam.

Preston steps out on the porch followed by the fucking devil.

"Well isn't this a coincidence." My blood boils and all common sense escapes me. I walk right up the steps and come nose to nose with Preston. "Looks like we have a fucking snake here."

Saint steps up to me. "What on the God's green earth is going on?"

"You know goddamn well, you fat fuck." I push him hard in the chest. "Since the day those colts stepped foot on our ranch we've had nothing but trouble. Burning down another man's barn is low, even for you."

I ball up my right fist and swing as hard as I can, make contact with his jaw and watch as he falls back. Preston catches him by the elbow and I hear his wife yelling in the background about calling the cops, but I'm beyond pissed.

"Our dad fucked up. Take it out on him, kick his ass, do what you got to do, but leave Silver Star out of this."

"Boy, you just made the worst mistake of your life."

I hear gunshots and turn to see Maverik taking out the windows of every single work truck on the place.

"Tell him to stop," Saint growls.

"Payback is a bitch, and every time something goes down at Silver Star you can bet your sweet ass we'll be right here paying you back."

"Merek Slatter, I suggest you back off right now. I'm the little fish in this whole racing world, and your daddy pissed off the wrong people. I'm just the messenger in all of this."

"What fucking ever." I take another swing and land another hard punch to the other side of his face.

Preston shoves me from the side and then that's when I really see red and let it all go. I start swinging with all I have until I see and smell blood. Marvel pulls me back.

"You're wasting your goddamn energy on the wrong people." Saint chuckles. "Your daddy fucked up big time. Selling a lame colt to a big racer and then tried to pay off his debt with counterfeit money, causing Louie to get locked up for five years. Louie is out and ready for payback, and he doesn't care if it's your dad or daddy's ranch."

"Who the fuck is Louie?"

"Son, after this little mess here today, I have a feeling you'll find out sooner than later."

The sound of cop sirens get closer and I rip myself from Marvel's hold.

"Well, tell Louie my dad doesn't own a ranch." I turn to walk down the steps and don't believe a fucking word that just came out of his mouth. "My dad did tell me that your old lady was one fine lay."

"You son of a bitch." I feel the vibrations on the steps and know he's coming for me and step to the side, pushing him down to the grass, and then start raining all sorts of punches on him. This time I'm pulled off the bastard by a cop, handcuffed, and stuffed in the back of a cop car alongside of Maverik and Marvel.

***

I cover my eyes as I walk out into the sun, Challis jumps into my chest before I see her nearly knocking me to the ground.

"I'm so pissed at you." Her lips are on mine kissing the ever-loving piss out of me. I wrap my arms around her waist and never want to be without her for another night.

Every time Maverik or my ass has landed in jail, Granddad makes us stay the night. It's his way of saying you dumbasses.

"Your granddad is in the truck. I stayed the night with him last night. Your mom took off to stay with her parents for a while."

"Okay." I walk backwards toward the truck, keeping Challis pressed up to my chest and kissing her as we walk.

"I'm going to fall."

"I've got you."

She giggles into my lips. All of us climb into the truck. I settle into the driver's seat with Challis in the middle and then Granddad. My brothers are in the back, and I finally have the courage to lean forward on the steering wheel and look at my granddad.

"Well?" he asks.

"I went and beat the shit out of Saint and Preston."

"Preston?" Challis questions.

"And did it make anything better? Solve all of your problems?"

"No, Granddad, it didn't, but sure as hell made me

feel better."

"You know he's pressing charges."

"Sure do, and I'll do the same thing again when they fuck with Silver Star. I'm not going to let them get away with this shit."

He nods his head.

I start the engine and then rat out Maverik. "Mav shot all the windows out on the place."

"Goddamn, boys." Granddad pounds the dash and I knew that would get him fired up. He turns around and swats at Maverik in the back seat. I bust out laughing at the old man. "Since you were eight years old, Maverik, you've gotten into more trouble with that damn shotgun."

"Sorry, Granddad."

I turn to look at Maverik, who has a shit-eating grin covering his face. I know damn well he's not sorry but just being respectful.

"What about the colts?" Challis asks.

"We'll finish our job and wash our hands of the fucker," Marvel pipes up.

"We owe more money to whoever this Louie is," Maverik adds.

"Challis and I are going to hit the road, chase our titles, and send all of our paychecks back to you guys."

"We are?" She turns to me.

"We are going to save Silver Star, get you your first national title, and bring Wine Cup back to life."

"Okay." She nods.

"And I'd like to see the wedding happen before I die, Merek." Granddad pats Challis's leg.

Chapter 20

Challis

"How long have we been on the road, Merek?" I wipe the sleep from my eyes.

"Too damn long, babe."

"But how much longer until we get there?"

He reaches down and swats my ass. He hates it when I ask that, and I do it on purpose just to annoy him.

"You have two more rodeos and are sitting in the number four position going into the finals, Verde, so go back to sleep and rest up. It will be a tight push for us to make it."

I've gotten used to cutting it tight. It's never been a problem for me, but since Merek's event is always first it seems like we've done nothing but bust ass from one rodeo to the next.

"Are Maverik and Granddad going to make it?"

"Yeah, he called about twenty minutes ago and they're already there."

"Damn, nothing like being early."

"He has Granddad with him, that's why."

I chuckle and miss the old man like crazy. After the fire, he and I bonded quite well. We ate dinner at his house every single night until it was time to leave for the road. We've been gone nearly four months traveling all over and rodeoing.

"Do you think he's going to kick your ass when we tell him we eloped?"

"I'm not telling him. You are."

"Ha. Very funny, asshole."

I drift off to the day I said "I do" to Merek, and of

course in his cocky, badass mode, he did it in full fashion.

"Las Vegas has been good to us."

"Only because I'm with you." Merek shoots me a sly grin from the couch. He's naked with a blanket in his lap. We decided to break down and get a hotel, spending an extra night in Vegas to relax. It's something we never do since hitting the road to rodeo together. It's always go, go, go. I won't lie, it's been nice to relax an extra day with Merek.

I put down the stack of cash I'm counting from my winnings last night in the casino and raise my shirt over my head, exposing my skin and leaving me only clothed in my lacy panties. Merek is engrossed in an old western on the television, not paying attention to a damn thing.

"Merek."

"Yeah, babe."

I watch him mindlessly answer me without paying an ounce of attention to me.

"What are we going to do today?"

He shrugs this time and I'm fully convinced he didn't hear a damn word I spoke. The remote lays on the glass table next to him. I tiptoe up to him and grab it. Before he knows what's going on, I push the power button and finally have his attention.

"What in the hell?" He looks up to me.

"I was getting lonely in the big penthouse with all my money." I push away the blanket perched on his lap and then straddle him, wrapping my arms around the back of his neck.

He smirks at me. *"Your whole whopping one hundred and twenty five bucks."*

I try not to laugh and only shrug as I push my exposed skin up to his chest. "I asked what we were going to do today."

"Looks like you picked it already. Bedroom Olympics." He cocks an eyebrow in my direction.

"You got any skills, boy?"

He flips me over, pushing my back into the overstuffed couch and enters me without warning. His face is full of question, waiting on my answer as he works in and out of me, and I know what his damn motive is. He's trying to render me speechless and is beyond successful at it as only moans roll off my tongue.

He adds a bit more to the pot when he reaches down between us and works me closer to my release with his finger swirling around.

"Merek," I scream as I clutch onto him. My nails dig into his shoulder blades as I buck up, milking out the last waves of pleasure.

"Let's get married today." He grunts and releases inside of me.

"What?" I bolt up under his weight, knocking him off of me. I watch as he tumbles to the ground and knocks his elbow on the corner of the table.

A mixture of laughter and groans of pain escape as he rolls around on the floor. "I take that as a yes?"

I look down at him from the couch and can't help but smile at my badass boy lying naked on the ground. "It's a yes."

"Get dressed. We are going now before you change your damn mind on me."

"Naked?"

"Move, Challis."

I hustle to the bathroom before Merek has the

171

chance to slap my bare bum and squeal the whole way as I go. My fingers tremble as I lock the bathroom door. I know if I leave it open I'll have a visitor whose sole mission is to distract me and make me hopelessly delirious with his lovemaking skills.

"Ten minutes," he hollers from the other side of the door.

"Okay, okay."

Turning toward the mirror that covers the entire wall in the bathroom, I see a rosy-cheeked version of myself staring back at me. I look again, taking a longer and deeper stare and am amazed by what I see. A girl who has her life back, living out her dream, and in love. My green eyes sparkle back at me and I see my daddy's love in them. The love that planted my roots and turned me into this.

I move quickly to the side, not wanting to spiral down a path of sadness thinking about my dad, and I guess my wedding day. I tug up my jeans and toss on my white tank top.

"Merek, are you sure you want to do this?"

"Dead serious."

I pull on my favorite pair of Ferrini cowboy boots and open the door. Merek is standing right on the other side of it.

"Stalker." I joke but only joke to hide the fact he literally just took my breath away. The scent of his musky cologne hits me first and then his starched jeans and favorite black cowboy hat are next. He's a walking sexy billboard for every cowgirl's dream and he's about to become mine.

He guides me out into the hall and as we wait for an elevator I panic.

"Merek, I look like shit."

He growls at me then reaches over biting down on my bottom lip and drags it out until it makes a popping sound.

"Sexy as sin is all see, baby, and if the Elvis that marries us looks down at your tits, I'll hurt him."

The elevator opens and is filled with my loud laughter. We walk a couple of blocks until we spot the cheesiest of cheesy chapels with cupids, neon lights, and a life size Elvis lighting up the front.

"Challis, I'll give you a big fancy wedding."

"Puke." I drag him up the steps and into the red crushed velvet chapel. We both have a hell of a time being serious with the over the top theme.

As soon as Elvis starts the ceremony we both fall silent and listen closely repeating along and saying our I do's.

After a very long and heated kiss, Elvis speaks up, "Just a minute, sir, and we'll get you the songs you requested."

I give Merek a sideways stare and watch Elvis waddle back down the aisle. Where I'm sure any typical bride would be appalled, in this moment my life couldn't be more perfect.

"What's he talking about?"

"There are two songs that I want to dance with you to."

"Really?"

"Yeah." He bends down and kisses me again as Neal McCoy fills the room singing his song No Doubt About It.

"You're going and getting all romantic on me, Slatter."

He places one hand on my cheek and the other on my lower back. "To me, I married you the day in your trailer when I gave you my buckle. I'm just making it legal, baby."

I fall into him, letting him sway me back and forth to the song. "I love you, Champ."

Keith Whitley's When You Say Nothing At All *starts playing next, causing a steady line of tears to run down my cheeks.*

"This was my daddy's favorite song."

"I know." He winks down at me.

"How?"

"Tori. I told her I was going to make this official out on the road."

"It's perfect."

This will be as close as we get to being home and actually get to spend a few days in Sterling. It's only twenty minutes away from Silver Star.

I look up at Merek. "Do you think we'll have time to stop by Wine Cup on our way out from here?"

"Of course, baby."

Merek made good on his promise and brought my daddy home. The bitch had him moved to the public cemetery. I've visited him a couple of times back on the ranch. Marvel being the very savvy businessman and rancher has Wine Cup running with a thousand heads of cattle and is being managed by his best friend from high school, Tanner. He's a great guy and I know my dad would be proud as hell even though we're not running bucking bulls.

"I can't sleep now. How much longer now?"

Merek grabs my side and pinches it. I can't help the fit of laughter that ensues.

"Ask me again and I'll pull over this truck and beat your ass."

"Well, I do like it rough."

His phone keeps going off, and Merek tosses it to me.

"Here. Someone thought it was a good idea to teach Granddad how to text."

"Oh my God, really? Why hasn't he texted me?"

"Give him hell, Verde."

I waste my time by texting him all sorts of messages and emoticons and sing along to our music.

"God finally found a way to make you shut up. We're here."

I sit up and spot Maverik and Granddad sitting on his tailgate and I wave like an idiot. The Slatters have become my family and home. I bolt from the truck before Merek has the chance to park it and run straight to Granddad.

"Hey, Sissy."

"I've missed you guys so much." I wrap him up in a hug and kiss his cheek.

"You too, big guy." I give Mav a quick hug.

"Must say we've all missed you on Silver Star, Sissy."

I squeeze in between the two of them and love hearing them call me by my new nickname. Maverik passes me a beer.

"Cheers." Granddad holds his bottle up to mine.

"What are we cheering?"

"You marrying my grandson."

My eyes go big and I hear Merek laughing in the background.

"You two owe me one hell of a party back at Silver Star."

"Deal."

I take a long pull from the beer and toss my bottle

175

cap toward Merek, who settles between my legs.

"Gotcha."

The men erupt in laughter.

"He had me scared shitless to tell you." Granddad pats my leg.

"I'd never get mad at you, girl. Can you walk me to get a burger and a seat in the stands?"

"Sure can, handsome." I hop off the tailgate and hold my hand out to help him down.

"Spur the piss out of that bucker, son." He gives Merek a quick hug before we make our way to the food booth.

I turn quickly to Merek. "Hey, honey, will you get Teebaby out and tie him up before you go behind the chutes?"

He nods back to me. Granddad orders a couple of cheeseburgers and a Coke before I settle him in the stands.

"Quite the appetite there, tiger."

"Don't get these very often. Have to splurge."

I kiss him on the top of the head and make sure he has everything. He asks for a cute little gal and I just walk away shaking my head. I guarantee back in the day that man would've given Merek a run for his money.

To this day, I've never watched Merek ride and got over my ritual of pacing and singing and just focused on my horse.

"Hey, sweet baby boy." I pat Teebaby on the rump as I walk up to him and he spooks, jumping back and swinging his head around.

"What's wrong, boy?" I offer him a cookie and he doesn't take it.

I shake my head and wonder if all the constant

traveling is taking a toll on him, but in all honesty he's treated like royalty on the road. Merek has even become fond of him, spoiling him rotten.

I pull up each of legs to make sure nothing is irritating him, and that's when I hear Merek and Maverik's voices in the background. They're talking loud and laughing as they walk back from the chutes.

Teebaby blows up and knocks me back on the dirt, sending dust swirling everywhere.

"What's his deal?" Maverik asks.

"Merek, he's acting weird."

"I'm sure he's just ready to run, babe."

"No, he's acting super funny."

"Saddle him up and warm him up. He'll be fine."

I change my clothes quickly and then saddle up Teebaby. He seems much calmer, and when I offer him his cookie this time he takes it and nuzzles into my shoulder. I pat his cheek and kiss the top of his nose.

"You okay, baby?"

Of course, he doesn't answer, but I have an unnerving feeling something is up with him. I hop on him and begin to walk away but remember I didn't ask Merek what he scored. Tugging on Teebaby's reins, I stop him and feel him rear up underneath me.

"Something isn't right with that horse." I hear Maverik's voice.

"He's fine." Merek waves him off.

"Hey, Champ, what did you score?"

"Seventy-nine. Got a shitty horse."

"Ah, sorry, loser."

I kick Teeaby into a trot and head to the warm up pen. I let him go and run and feel him hitch every once in a while. It's almost like he's stumbling. They call for the barrel racers and I line up almost thinking to pull from the race, not liking the way he's acting, but as soon as we get into the line he starts stamping his feet and throwing his head in excitement.

"That's the Teebaby I know." I pat his mane and keep him checked until it's our turn. He's focused on the arena and I urge him on. Teebaby takes the first barrel perfectly. I sit up and guide him into the second barrel, he sits his ass down and takes it tight on our way to third and I feel him stumble again, causing me to lurch forward in the saddle. He doesn't see the third barrel and keeps running full speed toward the fence.

"Whoa. Whoa," I scream trying to get his attention, but he doesn't hear me and it's like my horse has lost all of his senses. I hear it before I realize what is happening. Teebaby's chest collides into the fence and I hear his front legs crack and rip as the collision happens. Then I feel myself being lifted up into the sky, and then everything goes black.

Chapter 21

Merek

It never gets old seeing my cowgirl take the arena and kick ass on the back of Teebaby. I've never told her, but every time she rounds a barrel I'm a bundle of nerves hoping it's a clean run. They've tipped a few barrels and lost a few rodeos but not very damn many.

I notice Teebaby stumble out of the second barrel and then kick it up a gear and completely miss the third one. Catapulting off the chute, I run out in the arena and can hear Challis trying to calm him down. Then in a flash I watch helplessly as he collides into the fence, sending her over into the steer pen.

"Medic. We need a medic. Fans please stay seated."

I run to Teebaby. He's writhing in pain and thrashing, and then look to the fence to Challis who's trying to drag herself to her horse.

"Stop, Challis. I've got him. Stay fucking still."

A timer jumps the fence and is at her side trying to calm her down, and that's where I want to fucking be is by her side, but I know she'd want me with Teebaby.

Maverik is by my side and stands up and hollers. "Call a vet."

"We need a vet to the arena. Again a vet to the arena. Fans please remain seated."

Teebaby continues to thrash and moan in pain. His front legs are covered in blood. Dust rolls up around us as I look for the cuts, and that's when I notice the large gash across his chest. My heart shatters for the horse and even more for my girl. She's inched her way up to the fence and has her hand on his nose trying to talk to him.

"Hey. Hey. Hey, baby, I'm here."

Her other arm has an exposed bone sticking from it as blood runs down the side of her face. I can't handle it any longer and leap over the fence, picking her up in my lap and getting her closer to her horse.

"Baby, it's okay. It's okay, sweet baby." She pats his face.

"Where's the fucking ambulance?" I roar.

"Merek, go help him, please. Help Teebaby." Challis sobs.

"I'm not leaving you."

"Merek." Her voice is filled with a wicked combination of pain and horror. "Help him."

Her one good hand leaves Teebaby and she starts pounding on my chest.

"Go, son." I look up to Granddad who takes his time kneeling on the ground. "I have her."

I hear his calm voice talk to her and tell her to focus on breathing. I jump the fence again and run into a lady who has a bottle and a syringe.

"My husband is the local vet and on the way but said to give the horse twenty cc's of this."

Without thinking or even asking what it was I give it to Teebaby and he instantly settles. I watch as his stomach slowly rises and falls while Maverik has his shirt off and pushed up against the nasty wound on Teebaby's chest, trying to stop the bleeding. The ambulance backs up to Challis and she's loaded on a stretcher.

"Maverik, don't leave his fucking side. I'm going with her."

The ambulance door begins to shut. "Please, let me

in. I'm her husband."

"Sorry, sir. Policy is no one can ride in the back besides the patient and us."

"I don't fucking care about policy."

Challis's boot begins to quake and then her whole body seizes.

"You need to move, sir, so we can get her medical attention."

"Merek." Granddad pulls me by the arm just enough and the two doors slam shut. "Take Maverik's truck. We'll take care of Teebaby."

"Nothing, and I mean nothing, can happen to that horse." I grip the top of my hat, feeling my whole world crumble beneath me.

"Wear your seatbelt and drive with sense. She'll be okay. Just a little beat up. That girl is tough as nails."

"She won't be okay if he doesn't make it. Fuck," I roar.

I nod to Teebaby who's beginning to thrash around again. Blood seeps through Maverik's shirt, and fellow cowboys offer up blankets to help stop the bleeding.

"Go, son."

I jump the fences and weave through different pens until I'm at Maverik's truck. My fingers grip the steering wheel, and for the first time in my life I can call on the man upstairs to watch over my wife and the love of her life, Teebaby.

As I drive through town, Maverik's warning about the horse not being okay plays over and over in my mind. That horse would never do anything to hurt Challis. He has a heart of gold and is wired to run barrels. Nothing would ever throw him off his game.

The hospital comes into view and my heart races

as I've never felt so damn helpless in my entire life. Tears threaten, but the sheer rush of panic and anxiety dam them back.

Rushing into the entry labeled ER I hear a man calling after me.

"Sir. Sir. Sir. You left your truck running."

Without turning, I yell back to him, "Well turn the fucker off."

The ER waiting room is packed as doctors and nurses buzz about everywhere.

"I'm looking for Challis Jones. She was just brought in."

"Just a second please, I'll go see if you can see her."

Saying her last name kills me. She's such a stubborn shit and wanted to keep her maiden name. It's one fight I should've fought harder to win.

"Only next of kin can see her right now."

"I'm her husband and she has no living relatives." I lie.

"Follow me please."

We pass several closed off rooms and some that are open. The place smells like death, the sounds going off around me help lighten my fears.

"Here you go."

"Challis." I push past the receptionist and get to her side. "Baby, how are you doing?"

She rolls her head and looks at me. They have her face cleaned up, but her left eye is rapidly swelling shut with black bruises already covering it. Her arm has a clear plastic bag over it.

Tears roll down her face. "How is he? How's my horse? I want to go to him."

"I know, baby."

"Granddad and Maverik are with him and will

travel to the vet. I told them not to leave his side."

"Why did that happen?"

"I don't know, baby, but the good news is it looks like your injuries are pretty minor."

"They are calling a surgeon to fix my arm." She rolls back to her side. "I'll die if anything happens to him."

I don't try to cheer her up or tell her otherwise because it's her reality and the cold hard truth. And I have no idea if Teebaby will make it or not. In all of my years on the ranch and at rodeos I've never seen a horse in such pain.

"Challis, how's your pain level?" A tall bald man walks in the door and sits next to her on a stool.

She just shrugs, not answering him.

I stand to my feet and hold out my hand. "I'm Merek, her husband."

"Nice to meet you."

"We are prepping the OR right now for surgery. She needs her arm set in place, and we are also watching some internal bleeding she has going on. She also has a severe concussion."

"Will I be able to go home tonight?" Challis asks.

"Oh no, we'll have you here for a few days. Your arm is pretty messed up, and we need to keep a close eye on your head injury."

She sits straight up in the bed. "I have to leave tonight. I have to get to Teebaby."

"Challis, I told you Maverik's with him. You just need to worry about you right now." I place my hand on her hip and squeeze it trying to offer up a bit of comfort.

She swings her legs over the side of the bed and fights to get up.

"Stop. Now." I feel like an ass for yelling at her and pushing her back down on the bed.

The doctor calls for a nurse to come in and I watch as they inject something in her IV.

Challis fights against me. I'm cautious of not wanting to hurt her arm, but she doesn't seem to care.

"Keep a good hold of her." The doctor nods to me.

Challis is wrapped up in my arms crying out Teebaby's name and trying to fight to get past me. Soon, I feel her melt in my arms as her head sways to the side.

"I gave her a little bit of a sedative. We need to try to do our best to keep her calm."

Carefully, I lay her back down in the bed and cover her up in her blanket. Dropping my forehead to hers, I finally let a few tears and fears flow down my cheeks.

"I love you, Challis Jones. You have no choice but to pull through this like you've done in everything else the rest of your life. Come back to me."

***

It's well after midnight and Challis is still in surgery. A nurse calls the waiting room every so often giving me updates. The last one was just a few minutes ago letting me know they are stitching her back up and the pins worked perfectly.

"How is she?" I look up to see a very exhausted Maverik and Granddad in the doorway.

"She's fighting, that's for sure. They're just finishing up her surgery now." Both men take a seat across from me. "She had to be sedated in the ER because she was trying to get out of the bed to go and be with Teebaby."

Maverik drops his head down and scrubs his face with his two palms. "It's not good, Merek."

"Fuck." My fist slams down onto the table.

"They did a blood test and he was poisoned, which explains his odd behavior. The vet said he'll never be able to run again due to the injuries to his front legs. He'll be lame forever."

"Was he a good vet? We need to get a second opinion."

"The horse is done, son," Granddad adds.

Once the words leave his mouth I know it's final. He's been around more horses than Maverik and I put together.

"This is going to kill Challis. Absolutely destroy her."

And out of all of today's events, this is the absolute worst. Challis might as well have lost her two legs.

Chapter 22

Challis

Three days caged in this room has nearly made me fucking insane. Any time I bring up Teebaby's name everyone avoids the topic, and then when I get insanely pissed I'm sedated.

Granddad hasn't left my bedside and no matter how enraged I get I haven't had the courage to tell him to fuck off and come clean, but I have on Merek several times. Tori visited a couple of times but couldn't handle me either. I see his face enter the room and my blood instantly boils. I know it's not rational, and it's definitely something I cannot control.

"Everything's packed. Let's go."

"Take me to him, Merek, no more pussyfooting around this."

"We are going straight to the vets."

He reaches for my arm and I pull it back. "I'm not fucking crippled, Merek. I can walk."

He throws his two arms up in the air and heads for the elevator. It's been like this since waking up from surgery. I can't control my temper, and he seems to be my favorite target.

"You should really take it easy on the boy. He's just as hurt as you and been worried like crazy."

"I know." Granddad takes my hand and the tears start rolling down my cheeks. I've had them pent up the last couple days and the dam breaks within me.

"He's had Maverik sit with your horse and he goes over and checks on him at least three times a day himself, and then has raced right back here to be

186

here for you." He gives my hand a gentle squeeze. "I know heartbreak, Sis, but there's no reason you should be treating him like this."

"I'm scared. I can't help it. I just keep blowing up every time I see him. It's like reliving the accident each time I see his face."

"Well, I hope you damn well know he'd give his life to erase that day for you."

We make it to the front of the hospital where Merek is leaning back on my truck with his arms crossed and gaze pointed downward. When he looks up, for the first time I see the toll this has taken on him.

"You're supposed to be in a wheelchair," he says walking up.

"She told the nurse to kick rocks," Granddad says.

I open the back door and take my time crawling up in the truck, which is more difficult than I thought with only one good arm and sore muscles everywhere. Merek looks back at me from the driver's seat with pain and heartache painting every one of his features. He's my husband and the man I love with my whole heart, but right now I don't need anyone touching me or looking at me with pitiful stares.

"How far away is the clinic?"

Merek doesn't answer me and neither does Granddad.

"Don't fucking ignore me, Merek." I slam my fist into the back of his seat. I feel the truck take a hard left. He slams it into park leaving behind a skid mark and jumps out.

"We're here, Challis. I didn't fucking do this to you. Do you hear me?" He walks off, not bothering to open my door. It takes me some time, but I'm able to hop down from the truck. I catch sight of my face in the side view mirror and cringe. My eye is still an ugly shade of black and green, but it's something in my facial features that even scares the hell out of me. I brush back my matted bangs and walk into the clinic.

"Hi, you must be Challis. I'm Dr. Westington."

"I want to see my horse now."

"I'd like to fill you in on some things before we go back."

"Are you fucking kidding me?" I throw my hands up in the air. "You can't talk while I see him?"

"Challis," Merek roars, anger oozing from his voice. "Sit down and shut the fuck up."

Reluctantly, I sit down and begin tapping my boot on the dingy white tile.

"Your horse was poisoned, and that's why he missed the barrel. He's suffered severe injuries to his front legs. It's my professional recommendation to have him put down. He'll only suffer the rest of his days and be severely lame."

Poison. Lame. Put down. All swirl together in my mind, nearly causing me to black out. I try to grip onto reality and hang in there.

"Take me to him now." I grab Merek's hand.

The vet nods to me and I follow him down a long hallway. Clutching hard to Merek's hand, I turn to him before entering the pen.

"I can't do this. I can't fucking do this, Merek." I bury my face into his chest. "I'd rather die than to have to face this."

"Your family is here. We'll always be here for you. It's your choice, Challis."

"Tell me what you think before I go in there."

"I'll support you with whatever you decide. Just know, Challis, you're never running barrels with him again. He's done."

My whole body sinks to the floor, but Merek pulls me back up and steadies me.

"He hears your voice, baby. He's whinnying for you."

"Well, look at that," the vet says, standing in front of the pen. "That's the most we've heard from this guy.

I round the corner with Merek pushing me from behind and gasp in horror. Teebaby is on his side and thrashing, trying to stand up and falling back down in pain. All of his white patches are stained blood red.

"Go, baby, he wants you." Merek pushes me from the small of my back.

Lurching forward I fall down onto him, kissing his face, cooing into his ear. As soon as I touch him he quiets and softly whinnies in my ear.

"I'm so sorry, baby. I have no idea what the hell happened."

I pat his cheek as my good arm wraps tightly around his neck. "He's going back to Silver Star with us."

The vet starts to talk but is cut off by Merek.

"You heard her. He's going home as soon as he can handle the ride. No fucking questions asked."

"He can travel today." Maverik steps in the stall. "I've been here the whole time and know exactly what he needs."

I look up to the vet. "He's correct. Teebaby can go home with the proper care. Just keep in mind he'll take a year or so to fully heal, and that's if he does."

"I'm not giving up on him. He pushed himself to

his limits all the time for me in the arena. I'm not giving up hope."

"C'mon, baby, let's get you home. Maverik will be behind us with Teebaby."

"Nope, I'm staying with him."

"Of course you are." Merek slams his fist into the gate. "Fucking woman, you're going to be the death of me. You just suffered a serious concussion and have pins in your arms. Just fucking listen for once, please."

I stand up and square off with Merek. "This is all fucking on you, Merek. You know it's just another retaliation from your dad's fucked up mess. I wouldn't be in this position if I never met you. So, don't you fucking dare tell me what to do and not to do."

I rip the buckle from my pants and shove it in his chest. "Here."

Then I turn back to Teebaby dropping to my knees, wrapping my arms right back around his neck. I don't give a fuck about the arm with a brace on it. I need to be here right now with my horse.

I hear Merek and Maverik bickering in the background but block them out and pour everything I have left in my tank into Teebaby.

"Sis." I look up into Maverik's dark brown eyes. "I'm staying here with you and taking you guys home. Merek is heading out."

"Okay." I lay my head down on Teebaby. "Am I making a mistake, Maverik?"

He takes a seat on a straw bale next to me and begins patting my back.

"Absolutely not. You need Teebaby in your life, but it's going to be hell watching your partner who was once a champion fight to walk."

Brushing my cheek against Teebaby's neck, I know Maverik is right, but it's a chance and fight I have to take.

"Thanks for always being here for me, Maverik."

"Anytime. Merek left this here for you. He didn't want to leave, but I told him you needed time."

He hands me the gold buckle, my wedding ring, and I take it and pull it into my lap.

"Why do I get so angry and take it out on Merek? It's like I see bright red when he enters the room."

"I don't know, Sis. I'm not a counselor."

"Will I ever get over this?"

"I don't know that either."

***

I've slept in the stall with Teebaby for the last week and only go in to take a shower and eat when I know Merek's out of the house. Every time I try to talk to him we end up fighting and saying nasty things to each other.

Teebaby is recovering well. He's able to stand up for long periods of time. Every single day his spirits get a bit better. It's his spirit that really gives me hope for the future. I know he'll never run again, but I just pray he can live out the rest of his days in lush green pasture pain-free.

A horse masseuse visits him every other day while I keep up on his antibiotic and other meds. He still loves his cookies, having his mane braided, and my company. My arm throbs, but is never enough to keep me from his side.

Merek paid Saint a visit with the same results as the previous time. He beat the shit out of him and landed himself in jail.

"Drinking already?" I ask as Merek enters the barn.

"What are doing here, Challis?"

"I'm trying to survive and coming to grips with the fact I'll never rodeo again. Apparently, it's all a big fucking party to you, Merek." I point at the beer bottle in his hand.

"I'll buy you a new fucking horse. We'll go back on the road again."

"It's all about money with you, Slatter."

He smirks and throws his beer bottle against the wall, sending glass in every direction. "Yep, all about money, Challis. I'd fucking do anything for you. My heart is yours. Fuck, I bought your daddy's ranch back for you...again, all about money."

"I can't just get on another horse, Merek. I'm sorry to disappoint. I'm a little more loyal than you."

"I'm just asking for my wife back."

I watch as he storms from the barn and then hear his truck peel out in the driveway. And just chalk this up to one more of our conversations we have on a daily basis.

I love the man and need him in my life, but I just don't know how to get over my anger to find my way back to him. It's a nasty thought that haunts me at night. What if I never find my way back?

Chapter 23

Merek

I'm over her and this fucking train wreck we both are in. It's fight after fight and everything is my fault. If my dad walked into this bar, I'd fucking strangle the bastard until he breathed his last breath. There's no proof Saint's crew did this, but it's the only damn possibility in my mind.

His gloat and smirk on his face haunts my sleep every night. The day I went to officially kick his ass for the second time he said, "I told you that you'd regret the day you came to my house."

That was all the fucking proof I needed. Challis acts as if my life is such a dream right now, but in fact it's a fucking living nightmare. I slam three more shots down without thought. Drinking has become my only saving grace. I try to order two more shots, but my tongue is thick and fat in my mouth and I'm unable to produce a single word. I wave down the waitress and feel my ass slip from the barstool and hit the wood floor. A muted wave of pain runs up my spine and then I hear my shirt rip as I'm pulled to my feet.

"His tab, please." I look over to see Maverik's boots and then up to his face to see he's fuming with fucking anger, and I can't help but laugh and know it's the wrong move. Jake tries to lick my face and it causes me to laugh even harder at the scene.

I'm dragged out of the bar as a set of knuckles connect with my jaw. The pain is dulled from the amount of alcohol flowing through my bloodstream. He throws me in his truck and I pass the fuck out.

193

Moments later, or who knows, it could've been hours, I feel my ass hit the gravel and then a kick to the ribs. I look up again to a pissed off Maverik.

"Challis, come take care of your husband. I'm done with this shit."

My head flops over to the side to see Verde walking out of the barn and I just laugh. There's no way in hell she fucking cares.

"What happened?" she asks as she nears me.

"The bar called again. He's trashed." Maverik pulls me to my feet as I sway back and forth. "Make a decision now, Sissy, this is getting fucking old and my brother deserves way better than this."

Maverik lets go of me and I fall back on the truck as I watch him walk away.

"It's okay, Challis, go tend to your horse and let your fucking hate brew for me." I try to stand and know I'm weaving from side to side. "Hope the barn is luxurious enough for your ass."

She reaches her hand out to me and I actually recoil from her, not wanting to ever feel her touch knowing it will only bring me more pain.

"I would've given up everything for you, Challis."

I take a step and eat shit and know I've hit rock bottom, but my selfish pride doesn't stop me from trying to get up.

"Thank you, Merek."

I look back at her and scowl.

"Thank you for loving me and being my Champ. I can't say sorry for what I'm going through because I can't even process it. Just imagine everything being ripped out from underneath you and yet you're expected to act as nothing ever happened."

"I never said that, Verde, and if you lost everything

guess you're counting me in on that. I'm leaving in the morning to rodeo." I stand this time and feel the effects of the booze rapidly wearing off. "Clearly, you don't need or want me."

"You are putting words into my mouth, Merek."

I stop, turn, and see for the first time in a very long time the feisty cowgirl who, deep down, is vulnerable as hell and doesn't have the first clue about asking for help.

"Then shoot it straight to me, Challis."

"You have rodeo still and two good legs under you. I fucking lost it all."

I walk straight up to her and see and feel her flinch. "You're my fucking everything and have left me."

I don't say another word as I walk straight into my house. It's dark and quiet and once again I'm left all alone. It shouldn't be anything fucking new but still hurts nonetheless. Stumbling around, I make my way to the shower and turn on ice cold water in the hopes of sobering up and not being fucking hung over when the sun rises.

I'm heading out to Fort Worth in the morning and clearly Challis could give two fucks. The ice cold water pricks at my skin and feels like a dozen needles attacking me all at once. The pain is a welcoming feeling. Feeling anything nowadays is something. I lean my head back and soap up my hair, closing my eyes and trying to forget.

A gust of air hits my back. I turn to look, and taking my breath away, see Challis on the outside of the shower with tears rolling down her bare skin. She's stripped naked.

"I'm lost and hurt. I love you, Merek, I really do,

but I'm fucking going crazy." She lifts a shaking hand to me. She can punish me the rest of her life with her stubborn ways, but there's one thing I'll never be able to do and that's turn away my girl.

I clutch on to her wrist and pull her under the assaulting water. Challis falls into my chest and lets out her racking sobs. My hands run all over her delicate skin, rejoicing in the touch and memorizing parts of her body. I know she's hurting and feels like she's lost it all, but I just don't know when the day comes that she'll walk away from me and never come back.

I've watched a shell of Challis the last couple of weeks and it's been painful, like a dagger to my heart, but nothing compares to this. The moment she finally opens up and crumbles under my touch. I reach back and turn on the warm water and then begin lathering her up. I'm not sure the last time she showered.

Her hair is matted, so I use extra conditioner to try to comb through the knots with my fingers. I use her razor and lather up her legs, taking my time. Once I have her clean, I turn off the water and lift her to my chest. Challis is an exhausted mess.

"I've never stopped loving you, Champ."

"It's okay. I'm not giving up."

She's dead silent as I dry her off on the countertop. I feel her fingers run over my shoulders and along my back, and it's as if she's doing the same thing of memorizing my parts.

"Want me to take you out to Teebaby?"

I'll sacrifice a broken heart before I ever make her choose between her horse and the future.

"Take me home."

I go out on a limb and lay her in our bed, tucking

her deep under our blankets, and then cuddling up next to her. I lie still next to her. Her heartbeat is the rhythm and song of my life—the sweetest song to my ears.

Challis rolls on top of me, pinning my arms back, I feel her settle down on me. It takes everything inside me not to groan out loud expressing the most thrilling sensation ever.

"Merek," she moans out as her rhythm and speed picks up. "Go on the road. Let me stay here and heal. I want to be better when you get back. I want to be okay."

It's like the most beautiful torture and I finally let a moan escape as I push up into her. I know I won't last long, so I clutch onto the sheets and focus on anything but Challis Jones.

"Bring home another gold buckle, Champ."

With the last of her words, I let go inside of her, and then yell her name in the most passionate mix of pain and pleasure I've ever experienced in my life.

Chapter 24

Challis

I roll over from the most blissful dream I've had in weeks and realize it wasn't a dream when my forearm hits the ice cold sheets. I sit up in a groggy state searching the room for Merek. Last night's events play in slow motion over and over in my head. I let him go, gave him the ticket to walk away and he did.

Racing around the house I holler out his name, and each time I realize that I lost him. The natural anger I've grown accustomed to controls me as I begin throwing shit around the house. I throw on his button up cowboy shirt and pull on my jeans as I race down the sidewalk looking for him or his truck or anything that might resemble Merek is still here and I find nothing.

"What's wrong, Sis?"

I look over to Granddad's porch where Maverik, Marvel, and Granddad sit sipping their morning cup of joe.

"He's gone." The tone of my voice is helpless and desperate, mirroring the same exact emotions I've been living on repeat.

Granddad nods his head. "He headed out this morning for a three month run on the road. Promised us all another gold buckle."

I sink into the misty grass, pissed beyond belief that I let the greatest thing ever happen to me slip away. He stayed by my side through fits and rages of temper. I even caught him in the stable talking to Teebaby and nursing his wounds even when I was at

198

my worst. I lost him forever.

Steadying my weakening legs, I stand and walk to the barn. I hear Granddad's voice.

"You okay, Sissy?"

"I'm good. Just going to do chores."

I feed Teebaby and then clean up the rest of the barn and find the hidden bottle of Crown. I take one sip and then three more before I finally collapse next to my horse and let him capture my tears. Teebaby lies there soaking up every ounce of my pain until my eyes drift shut.

***

My muscles are sore and stiff as I lift my head from Teebaby. His slow movements wake me and as soon as I sit up, he jumps up from the ground and heads to the feeder.

"Looks like someone is feeling better." I rub my aching head and notice the dusk settling in outside. I feed the barn and then head for the house with a rumbling belly. Granddad is in his rocking chair smoking on his pipe and Marvel is out in the pasture counting cattle. The quiet roar of the ranch settles my nerves and gives me the slightest hope of a future.

My career is over, but my life just started. I race into the house searching for my cellphone so I can call Merek. Haven't seen or touched the damn thing for weeks. After scouring every surface of the house and coming up empty, I reside to the porch with a longneck in my hand. The darkness settles in and I let the liquid calm my nerves.

A far-off set of headlights light up the long driveway to Silver Star. I steady my legs to go get Maverik. I just know it's the sons of bitches back again to torment us. As the lights get nearer so does the roar of the engine, and it's a familiar one. One I've heard in the past.

It's Merek. He skids in front of the house sending gravel flying in every direction. He jumps out as I stand to my feet. Before I can get a word out, he's next to me and lifting me in the air.

"I can't leave you. Rodeo is nothing without you. The buckles and fame are nothing compared to having you by my side, Verde."

"I'm sorry."

My face is lifted up to his. "You have to let me help and be a part of this too. I love Teebaby and you. If you keep shutting me out it won't work."

"I know." I bury my face in his neck, inhale his scent, and remember all the good times we've had together and how he stood by me through everything—good and bad.

"I'm laying down the rules, Challis."

His hands land on my face and he pulls me up to look at him.

"Merek, I'm so sorry. I just don't know how to react or let out all the anger. You still get rodeo and the sport you love."

"Shut up and listen to me, Challis." He places a quick kiss on my lips and I lurch forward, savoring the sensation of his lips on mine. Deepening the kiss and soaking up everything of the man who owns my heart.

He pulls back from me and tightens his grip on my face.

"Shit is going to change around here. You'll sleep in my goddamn bed every fucking night with me. No matter how damn hard of a day you've had."

I nod and whisper, "I want that."

"Two, you'll rodeo again. I'll give you the time you need to heal and we'll always keep Teebaby. He's ours. He's like our first child, but you'll rodeo again, and one day you'll be teaching our daughter to run barrels."

He waits for my response, but I can't find one, and realize it's because I don't even have the courage to try to look for one. It's scary to even think about loading up a trailer and heading down the road to a rodeo with Teebaby left in the stable. But what's even a more spine-chilling thought is losing Merek forever. Guilt, regret, and self-pity have to all come second to me loving my husband and myself again.

I slowly begin to nod my head up and down. "I don't want to lose you. I'll do anything for you, Merek, just don't give up on us."

"Third." His stern voice causes my knees to go weak. "We will fight and we will love. We are both passionate people, there's no doubt about that, but we can't keep doing this."

"Doing what?" I whisper.

"Destroying each other."

"I'll do anything to be with you, Merek, anything. I need you in my life." I step back leaning on the white railing of the porch. "Last night your touch reminded me of us and everything I love about life. When I woke up and you weren't there it reminded me of everything I hate about life. I choose you."

"What are you trying to tell me, Verde?"

I know he's pushing me to talk out my emotions and feelings. It's something I just don't do until I'm pushed all the way.

"I'm saying that I'm fucking scared, have lost hope,

but know without a doubt I need you in my life. There's no other option. I love you."

He nods his head, pushes back his cowboy hat, and leans into me. "I love you too."

Chapter 25

Merek

"You kids hungry?"

Granddad's voice breaks into my thoughts as I lean into Challis. My lips brush hers. My plan of attacking her lips and hauling her off to bed is put on hold. Challis accepts Granddad's invitation and it doesn't shock me, as I know eating dinners with him is her favorite part of the day when her head was screwed on straight.

She bounds from our porch, dragging me across the grass to his porch. It's like I'm her newfound trophy and she's ready to show it off. The simple action makes me feel more at home than anything ever has. The smell of the ranch, the smile on Challis's face, and Granddad's voice reassures me I made the right decision turning around on highway twenty-one. Rodeo and riding fuel me, the gold buckles are sweet, but living without Challis and leaving our story wide open is something I couldn't face.

Maverik told me not to leave and then called me once I did. He told me he wouldn't be by my side in the hospital when the wreck came that would end my career and possible life. He told me to go home and take care of my wife. I'll never tell the man how damn wise he is and how much more of a father figure he is to me than our own dad.

"Mmmmm...Granddad's famous chili." I watch as my girl digs into the large silver pot on the stove and don't miss the smile that covers my granddad's face.

She scoops us all out a bowl and even sets plates

for Marvel and Maverik. When she settles into her normal seat next to me, I realize that I haven't been able to take my eyes off her.

"I'm sorry." She pauses, covering her mouth.

"For?" Granddad asks.

"For not making cornbread like I always do when you make this."

"Challis, I'll only forgive you if you can forgive yourself." He covers her hand and I see a single tear roll down his cheek. "I never quit loving my Maggie and let me tell you we fought worse than you two, but in the end we loved harder."

The front door opens and slams shut, and when I look up I see my two brothers hanging up their hats on the coat rack by the door. Jake runs over to Challis, who fills his water bowl and food dish and then kneels down to pat his head and love on him. I need to buy the damn girl a pup.

Marvel unbuttons his long sleeve shirt, tossing it to the floor, and then heads off to the bathroom to wash up. Maverik is dressed in his town clothes and I don't miss the wink he sends my way with pride covering his face.

He settles next to Granddad in the same chair he's claimed since we were little. Challis rises from the table, dishes out two servings of food, and places them on the table. Maverik catches her hand before she steps back from the table.

"This is the Slatters. Us five. We will bring the ranch back to life ridding all of the debts and scandal clouding us." Marvel nods from the end as he exits the bathroom and grabs the jug of milk from the fridge. "We'll never give up on each other. We are a family."

Marvel settles into his chair and pours his extra large glass of milk. "What about Mom?"

"She had to leave. Her nerves couldn't handle any more stress. It's us. We're the Slatters and nothing will hold us back. We each will each experience our difficulties and time of darkness." I don't miss the extra squeeze he puts on Challis's hand. "But we are all here, no matter what."

"Amen." Granddad raises his glass of sweet tea.

"I'm in." Marvel raises his milk.

Challis bends over and kisses his temple. "Thank you."

I grab the frosty longneck in front of me. "When did you become so smart, asshole?"

The room erupts in laughter. Maverik tosses a fork at me, Marvel shakes his head as he devours his food, and Challis leans into me, soaking up the moment not touching her chili. We've all found our home.

Looking to each face surrounding me, I know that a gold buckle would never amount to anything without them in my life. Our table may be tiny, but our hearts and passion are fierce. We are the Slatters.

THE END

Find out who is behind the scandal in book #2 of the Silver Star Ranch Series. Maverik Slatter's book will be out in Jan. 2016. Enjoy Chapter 1

Rules of the Ride
Book #2
A Silver Star Novel

Chapter 1

Maverik

Splitting pains shoot around in my head, mouth dry, and a nauseous feeling already swirling around in my gut...yep, drank way too much last night. Rolling over in bed, my arms land across the warm skin of another body. Peeling my eyes open I see Ella in all her naked glory with her messy blonde hair sprawled across the pillow and my sheets.

"Fuck," I grumble trying to sit up in my bed, throwing my feet to the floor. Jake looks up at me with that face saying, *"You're screwed, man."*

Looking down, I'm naked as the day I was born, and as the events of the night before play out in my head, I realize I am fucked beyond belief. I finally gave into Ella, and now it looks like another ten years of heartache once she climbs in her fancy little sports car and drives away.

"Mav." I turn to see her rustling around in the sheets and then her baby blues look up at me. "Come back to bed."

Her tattoo dances up the side of her ribs and I don't think I'll ever get tired of staring at it. I had no idea she got it the day she left town. My name in western font goes from right underneath her armpit down to the top of her hips. Then my mind goes back to that vicious cycle and anger begins to boil up in me. She left me. Actually she chose to leave years ago, and I've let her right back into my life.

Hell, not only life, but my heart, bed, and soul.

Her palm brushes down my back and it's something about her touch that I'll never be able to let go of. The day I ran into her weeks ago in town, I should've turned and walked away, but like a fool I stared at her.

I feel the bed dip and then her arms drape around my neck with her breasts pressed up against my back. Her lips play with the lobe of my ear. My hand automatically goes to the back of her head, wrapping my fingers into her blonde locks.

"What's bothering you, Mav?"

I shake my head side to side. "Nothing."

"Then how about you lay back down with me?"

"I need to get an early start with Merek and Challis's reception today."

Yes, Granddad finally convinced the two assholes to have a wedding reception on the ranch. It's something he wanted and set Marvel and myself down and told us he'd whip our asses if we eloped. He explained he only let Merek do it because he knew Merek would do whatever in the hell he wanted.

Cold air sweeps across my back as Ella falls back onto the bed. I twist to see her covering her front with my sheet and that sad look that covers her face.

"I get it."

"Ella," I yell standing up to my feet and dragging my hands through my hair. "What in the hell are we doing here?"

She shrugs, with tears streaming down her cheeks. "I love you, Maverik."

"You don't love me. You love being with me and what we used to be, but you'll have no problem hopping in that fancy sports car of yours in one week and bolt from me once again." My fist goes straight through the drywall.

Out of the corner of my eye, I see her jump back further into bed and feel like an even bigger asshole, if that's possible. Staring down at her bright blue eyes, I realize that I'm already gone and have no chance of survival with Ella back in town.

I drop to my knees on the side of the bed, grip her thighs, and tug her toward me until she's straddling my torso. Tears stream down her face and she does her best to hide them from me with her long hair.

"I'm sorry." I tilt her chin up. "Ella, let's just focus on the reception today."

She takes a moment to gain her composure before she speaks. "Who says I'm leaving this time?"

"Nothing keeping you here."

Her hand touches my bare chest and then drifts over to my beating heart. "I want this, Maverik."

My phone goes off. I twist toward the nightstand and take the call.

"It's Challis," I whisper.

"Maverik."

"Yeah?"

"I'm freaking out. The DJ isn't here and the dance floor is all wrong. Someone left the irrigation on out by the pond and everything is swamped."

I interrupt her, "Slow down, Sis. Where's Merek?"

"He's picking friends up at the airport. I have a hundred things to do."

She continues to frantically ramble on in panic mode and I wonder if she'll ever realize that we'll always have her back. Calling me is one huge step for the feisty little shit. She generally bottles everything up until she explodes in a fit of anger.

"It's not funny," she yells as I laugh on my end of the phone.

I stand and look for my clothes. "I'll be right over. I need breakfast and a pile of ibuprofen."

"Okay." I hear a loud clatter in the background. "Granddad is here trying to help. He cooked up breakfast."

"Be there in a minute, Sis."

Ending the call, I toss my phone down onto the bed next to Ella.

"So, that's it, Maverik?"

"What do you want, Ella?" I ask as I pull on my pants trying to keep my balance.

"I want you." She stands, still covering her naked body.

Before I pull up the zipper on my jeans, I go to her, spinning her around and pinning her against the wall. I plant both of my palms on the wall framing her face.

We're so close I can feel her breath on my skin and damn near taste her sweet lips.

"I've wanted you for forever and that never stopped you from walking away from us. You've been gone for nearly a decade."

"How many times can I say sorry, Maverik, before

you'll forgive me?"

"I have my family and this ranch. They come first in my life. They've never walked out on me for bigger and better opportunities like you did." I step back before I find my lips on hers. "I'll see you at the reception tonight if you'd still like to be my date."

As the rage tears through my body, I still love the woman and would do anything to make her stay here with me or just lose myself in her until she leaves once again, but I listen to my brain for once and fight for me. I don't just want Ella Francis for a couple of weeks. I want her for a goddamn lifetime and am ready to force her hand.

Acknowledgements

As always, I have to tip my hat to my readers and friends who inspire me every single day to keep writing. Without your support these characters would never be born. Your encouragement goes a long ways from brightening my day to giving me strength to carry on with my dreams. Thank you so damn much.

Social Media Links
Website: www.hjbellus.com
Facebook:
https://www.facebook.com/AuthorHjBellus
Goodreads:
https://www.goodreads.com/author/show/7079478.H_J_Bellus
Twitter: https://twitter.com/HJBellus

Next Release From HJ Bellus
The Hunted
A Romantic Suspense With a Twist
August 2015

Merek & Challis Playlist

These two were on the road a lot together and developed quite the collection of good ol' country music. I hope you enjoy it. I know it's been on repeat since this project started.

Drink In My Hand- Eric Church
(Merek's Theme Song)
Heart Like Mine- Miranda Lambert
(Challis's Theme Song)
Lonely Eyes- Chris Young
(Night in the bar when Merek meets Challis)
A Guy Walks Into a Bar- Tyler Farr
(Night in the bar when Merek meets Challis)
No Doubt About It- Neal McCoy
(Merek & Challis's song)
Tomorrow- Chris Young
Neon Light- Blake Shelton
Sangria- Blake Shelton
Girl Crush- Little Big Town
Say You Do- Dierks Bentley
Goodnight Kiss- Randy Houser
How Country Feels- Randy Houser
Boots On- Randy Houser
Sparks Fly- Taylor Swift
Friday Night- Eric Paslay
Diamond Rings and Old Barstools- Tim McGraw
Give Me Back My Hometown- Eric Church
Hell On The Heart- Eric Church
Good Hearted Woman- Waylon Jennings & Willie Nelson
Take Your Time- Sam Hunt
Night Train- Jason Aldean

Bottoms Up- Brantley Gilbert
Bad Blood- Taylor Swift
Hurt Somebody- Dierks Bentley
Every Mile a Memory- Dierks Bentley
I Hold On- Dierks Bentley
Felt Good On My Lips- Tim McGraw
She's My Kind of Rain- Tim McGraw
Get Your Shine On- Florida Georgia Line
Round Here- Florida Georgia Line
Cruise (REMIX)- Florida Georgia Line feat. Nelly
Get Your Shine On- Florida Georgia Line
Holy Water- Big & Rich
Save a Horse- Big & Rich
Rollin'- Big & Rich
We Are Tonight- Billy Currington
Cowgirls Don't Cry- Brooks & Dunn
Back- Colt Ford with Jake Owen
Every That Glitters- Dan Seals
All Over The Road- Easton Corbin
Dirt Road Anthem- Jason Aldean
Church Pew or Bar Stool- Jason Aldean
Just Passing Through- Jason Aldean
Feel That Fire- Dierks Bentley
Come a Little Closer- Dierks Bentley
Free and Easy- Dierks Bentley
Straight Tequila Night- John Anderson
Broken Lady- Larry Gatlin & the Gatlin Brothers
Goodbye Lady- Micky and The Motorcars
Like A Wrecking Ball- Eric Church
Already Gone- Sugarland
Halfway Down- Patty Loveless
Just a Fool- Christina Aguilera with Blake Shelton
Unhappily Married- Pistol Annies
Give in to Me- Garrett Hedlund & Leighton Meester

Heads Carolina, Tails California- Jo Dee Messina &
Tim McGraw
Ain't In It for the Money- Micky and the Motorcars
It Ain't Easy- Jason Aldean
Gonna- Blake Shelton
Ready to Roll- Blake Shelton
If My Truck Could Talk- Jason Aldean
Days Like These- Jason Aldean
Why Don't We Just Dance- Josh Turner
Riser- Dierks Bentley
The Only Way I Know- Jason Aldean with Luke Bryan
Love Like Mine- Nashville Cast
Even If It Breaks Your Heart- Eli Young Band
Drinking Class-Lee Brice
Her Man- Gary Allen
The One- Gary Allen
It Would Be You- Gary Allen
Nothing On but the Radio- Gary Allen
Every Storm- Gary Allen
Pieces- Gary Allen
Right Where I need to Be- Gary Allen
Best I Ever Had- Gary Allen

Made in the USA
Charleston, SC
20 September 2015